Carmel Bird grew up in Tasmania, and now lives in rural Victoria. A most exciting and original writer, Carmel has published novels and short fiction, essays, children's books, and manuals on writing, as well as anthologies of stories and non-fiction.

www.carmelbird.com

Author's Note

I am grateful to the Australia Council for the Arts,
which awarded me a Writing Fellowship in 2010.
My Hearts Are Your Hearts is one of the projects I was able
to pursue as a result of the Fellowship.

SPINELESS WONDERS *Fiction Plus* Series

In this series we present collections of short Australian fiction with accompanying reflective essays by their authors. Designed to be enjoyed by lovers of creative literature, this series is an indispensable resource for writers, students, and anyone interested in understanding fiction from a writer's point of view.

First Published in 2015
Copyright Carmel Bird 2015

Spineless Wonders
Sydney

ABN 98156041888
PO Box 220
Strawberry Hills NSW 2012
www.shortaustralianstories.com.au

Edited by Bronwyn Mehan
Cover Design and Internal Design by Sandy Cull, gogoGingko
Cover Photograph by Griff Clemens
Typeset in 11.5/15pt Granjon by J&M Typesetting

Printed and bound by Lightning Source Australia

National Library of Australia Cataloguing-in-Publication entry
808.3

My Hearts Are Your Hearts/Carmel Bird

First Edition
Paperback ISBN 978-1-925052-21-3
Ebook ISBN 978-1-925052-08-4

MY HEARTS ARE YOUR HEARTS

Twenty new stories and their origins

Carmel Bird

CONTENTS

‘If you play your cards right you can go to sleep
and wake up with somebody else's heart.’
CARRILLO MEAN,
Marvels of Modern Medicine

‘We make fiction because we are fiction.’
RUSSELL HOBAN,
The Moment Under the Moment

BODY PARTS

MY HEARTS ARE YOUR HEARTS

In the Beginning

In one of the tents at Adelaide Writers' Week, Antony Elmer read from his latest novel, answering questions from a large audience of keen journalists and adoring fans. It was hot in the tent, there in the Pioneer Women's Memorial Gardens, and Antony sweated, the audience sweated, but it was worth it. He was brilliant. In another tent, Viviana Vincent did much the same, ditto the journalists and fans, except while her audience also poured with sweat, Viviana appeared cool (also calm and collected). Antony's novel, his seventh, was what is called 'literary', and it concerned a murder in Oxford in the 1990s. Viviana's was the latest in her Venus McVicker romances. The audiences in the two tents were different. Antony's lot was drawn from what is called the intelligentsia, and was clearly male, fellows packing down with the big boys. A smattering of women, mostly middle-aged. Viviana's people were predominantly women, women of all ages, their faces alight with excitement at being so close to the darling of their reading groups and book clubs. Antony's books sold very well, were warmly reviewed in all the best papers and journals, won prizes; Viviana's sold in fantastic numbers. They were ecstatically reviewed (in women's magazines). They did not win prizes.

<u>Who is Antony?</u>

Antony Winston Elmer was born in Canterbury in 1949. At Oxford he studied Medieval History. He has been married three times, his current wife being the celebrated TV presenter Minki Sackville. He has four sons and three daughters (the youngest daughter is screen actress Leaf Bath-Dickens). Three of his novels have been short-listed for the Booker Prize. Two have been made into films: *The Clear Spring* and *The Mourning of Exiles*.

<u>Who is Viviana?</u>

Viviana Maria Vincent was born in Hobart in 1960, named after her mother's favourite aunt. 'It's a lovely old-fashioned name, darling, a romantic name. Your great aunt was a very romantic lady.' The name was tailor-made for a writer of romance, and, as fate, luck, or destiny would have it, that's what Viviana became. Her Venus McVicker novels took off, and Viviana was a success, a sensation, a star. Fortunately she had a heart-shaped face, a dazzling smile, long lustrous chestnut curls, long long legs, a lithe and seductive body. A lilting speaking-voice. A certain wit and charming manners. Clothes loved her, the camera loved her also. She was a true gift to any publicist.

She lives, her biography will tell you, in a rambling Georgian house overlooking the Derwent River on the outskirts of Hobart in historic Tasmania. With, it says, her husband (childhood sweetheart – can this be true? It is). Her children (a film-maker, a barrister and a sculptor) all live overseas. There is soon to be a baby granddaughter. (Imagine!) Viviana and husband Will also have a most beautiful house in Provence. The children are called Xenia, Yvonne and Zac. VWXYZ. Yes. Please don't give this a moment's thought.

The Novels

The latest *St Valentine's Day* was heralded on long banners in airports across the world, alongside, as it happened, banners shouting out Antony's title *Carnival of Lust*. When people stopped at the airport bookshops, the two books were dropped into separate bags, and they left on different arms. Supermarkets discounted both. It has to be said that *St Valentine's Day* outsold *Carnival of Lust* in the supermarkets. But the latter novel was going to win important prizes; the former, naturally, was not. Viviana has read several of Antony's novels; Antony would not be seen dead reading any of hers.

In the Book Tent

After the sessions in the tents, Viviana and Antony (she in pale green silk and sandals, him in white jeans, white shirt, pale blue linen jacket, bright pink face and panama hat) were shepherded by their publishers to the table in the Book Tent where they would sign the books bought by their fans. They sat side by side, some distance from each other, and each had a glass of chilled champagne. Queues of readers wanting books signed snaked round the tent and out the door. Viviana's queue was longer than Antony's, but not by so very much. Some equal opportunity readers carried both books, and would lean across from one writer to the other for a signature. I probably don't have to tell you that Viviana signed her books in deep juicy pink, with a fountain pen. Antony also signed with a fountain pen – his ink was black. Velvety black. Both pens were Mont Blanc. His was the Mark Twain Limited Edition; hers the Boheme Pirouette Lilas. (You'd better believe it.)

All this is as it should be, as is to be expected. Viviana's publisher had provided a large silver bowl, and in the bowl were chocolate hearts, covered in scarlet foil. These were for Viviana to offer to her fans when they handed her a book for signing. When Antony reached across and slid the bowl towards himself, then offered the hearts to his readers, Viviana (surprised) simply smiled and said: Be my guest. My hearts are your hearts. (She really hated bad manners, and his were pretty bad.) I think I said Viviana's smile was dazzling. Antony caught the *ping!* of it right between the eyes, and that, as far as Antony was concerned, was that. His biography might not say so, but perhaps it suggests the idea that Antony was susceptible to a pretty face and a long leg and a dazzling smile. Chestnut curls were also very nice. He wasn't good at telling one perfume from another, but the miasma of 'Josephine' that drifted across to him from Viviana was having a bit of a funny effect on him too. He rather liked her ghastly colonial accent, in a way.

After the Book Tent

When all that was over, the two stars and their publishers returned to the hotel. Showered and changed into fresh cream shirt (him) fresh grey cotton sundress and small diamond earrings (her) they found themselves (fate, luck, destiny etc) side by side again in the lounge, drinking chilled (everything was chilled, really — this was, after all, Adelaide in summer) white wine and nibbling from bowls of nuts. Publishers and publicists and journalists and fans had all melted away. You can't count on a fan or two not turning up again, but for the time being Viviana and Antony were in a soft leather sofa world of their own.

Now I haven't told you before about the fact that Viviana, for all the views of the Derwent River and the adorable house in Provence, sometimes felt — how shall I put this — *bored* by the very idea of Will. Particularly when she was alone at a festival in the company of a wolf like Antony. (I believe I suggested he was a wolf.) Yes, this princess of romance was not above slipping upstairs with a troubadour of the Oxford college. You are saying – oh, for heaven's sake, she's fifty something and he's ten years older. *What* is going on? You must try not to be ageist. They make rather a handsome couple there in the subdued glow of the hotel lounge, in their nice fresh clothes, with, now, a bottle of *Mister Big Mouth Pinot Grigio* on the low table between them. Viviana ordered it as a joke – Antony chuckled. It was a good joke, and a very nice drop.

In the light of, in the face of their differences – and these were several, not least the nature of their writing, and their idea of manners – they were getting along quite nicely. Antony is in the habit of coming straight to the point. No use wasting precious time on beating about the bush. We could have dinner later? He says. And she says – Yes let's have dinner later. And he says – You want to come up to my room? She thinks for a minute and says – Well, why don't you come up to mine? When we've finished this?

So they finished the bottle and went up to Viviana's room. They ordered champagne which fortunately came with lots of nuts and olives and things on skewers. And he said – *St Valentine's Day* – is that about a massacre? And she said – *Carnival of Lust* – is that about Venice or about animals madly mating in the Adelaide Zoo? (I never said either of these people was *particularly* witty.) He hadn't expected that. He said – once I won the Bad Sex award you know. And she said – Was that for a book or for some terrible thing you did in bed? He said – Probably a bit of both. And she said – Well I think you can have the Good Sex Award today. And afterwards they had a long bath together and drank the champagne and nibbled on the nuts and things. They didn't ever have dinner, but they ordered some of the tandoori chicken open sandwiches for which the hotel was renowned – and Tony also gobbled up some of the chocolate bars from a basket on top of the mini-bar.

Now when Viviana indulged in these episodes, she thought very little of it all, and returned refreshed to Will in the lovely old house overlooking the Derwent River. But Antony was, in fact, more romantic than she was. He wanted to see her again. Maybe in Provence some time? Maybe one day soon in the house overlooking etc etc. But after breakfast which they shared in the sitting room of Viviana's suite, before some journalists were due in her room and also in his, she said no to Provence and no to the house on the Derwent, and said she had to hurry now. The hair-dresser was coming. So she kissed him softly at the door. And handed him a small paper bag containing six chocolate hearts, wrapped in scarlet foil.

BACK TO THE WOMB

Once upon a time. Listen.

First, how about a question.

If you were a young woman of, say, twenty-seven (the optimum age, so I've been told, for conceiving, carrying, delivering a child), and there you were facing the O&G across his desk, him in crisp blue shirt (you see him from a bit above the waist, up), silver hair, twinkly-twinkly eyes, you in white linen jacket with amazing dark resin buttons, new short-short haircut, unimaginably long silver earrings, and he says something along the lines of:

'Well, as you know, the past tests indicated the absence of a uterus. However, it is not all bad news. It could be possible for you to bear a child, providing we can access a suitable uterus, suitable for implantation.' – what would you do?

I can see you're not quite comfortable. You're not the only one.

Youngwoman (Y) felt her head spinning. Her uncle had had a heart transplant. Lived for fifteen years afterwards. Her boyfriend's brother had had a kidney, donated by his cousin. Transplants were therefore not unknown to Y, and she had heard tell of the medical possibility of receiving a uterus, but the idea of it, suddenly out there on the table in front of O&G was, she found, breathtaking. She was dizzy, and O&G suggested she lie down again. She lay there on the white sheet for a long time in the gentle silence of his room, and the nurse brought her a cloudy white sweet drink. O&G spoke to her from time to time. There were the words 'access' and 'suitable'. Sometimes O&G used the term 'womb' which was a word that Y found much more disturbing, somehow, than uterus. It rhymes with 'tomb', for one thing, and it hangs in the air, before the comma, when you say 'Blessed is the fruit of thy womb, Jesus'. Y was a Catholic, and she had prayed for a medical solution to her dilemma. Here it was. Transplant of a Suitable Uterus.

Y had been examined by O&G when she was sixteen. The doctor was seeking an answer to the question as to why Y was not menstruating. The result of the examination was the establishment of the fact that Y had been born without a uterus. This condition was, apparently, not uncommon, although no reliable statistics are available. At the time of the discovery of the absence, there was no imagined solution. The only miracle would be a Lourdes type miracle, and Y had no ambition for such a dramatic intervention. As well as being Catholic, the family was a great believer in the wonders of the medical profession. Y's mother was a nurse and her father was a successful manufacturer of prosthetic limbs. So here was the miracle of the medical solution, the proposition of a transplanted uterus.

There are other matters hanging on all this, other things to attend to. There's the question of not having children out of wedlock – so there will have to be a wedding. (Y was conceived before her parents were married, Y being known at the time as The Consequences. The priest at the little church of the Infant of Prague – he was affectionately known as Father Shotgun, did a brisk trade in weekday weddings in the sacristy. For a couple of Confessions and a nice big donation to the Mission Fund, he was more than happy to oblige.) Y's case was, you can see, different from that of her mother. Y and her boyfriend IT (works in Information Technology) could (and did) engage in as much sexual congress as they liked with no Consequences. Unless, obviously, Y were to access a suitable uterus, in which case Y and IT would best be wed in advance, all things considered. IVF would be necessary – sperm from IT, egg from Y, resulting foetus implanted in the transplanted uterus. It occurs to me that they'd better check out the fertility of IT before they tie the knot. You've heard of irony. You know about twists of fate. (Sigh of relief. They did check him out, and all was well.) In spite of having no uterus, Y had a healthy pair of ovaries. IT was keen to marry and have children (well, to begin with, a child).

Yes – now – in this day and age, it may be possible to conceal some medical secrets, but not, I imagine, the transplant of a uterus. I think (I could be wrong about this) that at least close family members are in on it all. Particularly when the donor of the necessary organ is the mother of the donee (I checked for a better word here, but there doesn't seem to be one. So Y is the donee.) Take the womb away from the mother and give it to the daughter who knows it well from the inside. Yes, take it, said Y's mother. Take it with my blessing. Life is a matter of give and take – and hope and trust – and a certain amount of philosophy.

Y's mother checked it out with Y's father who was cool with it. (Wait until he hears about the 'chunks' of blood vessels that will have to be removed from the body of Y's mother, and the risks to the life of the donor. He might not be so gung ho then.) And although the news was received by the family of IT with some bewilderment, they agreed that it was generally a 'good idea'. Y will have to take lots of medication during the hoped-for pregnancy. Fine. Then there will be the business of IVF. This can be long and wearing and even unsuccessful. And if she has two pregnancies, the uterus will be removed after the second one. Fine.

So things were going along well, and O&G was assembling a formidable team of surgeons from all over the world. He was preparing Y and her mother physically and emotionally for the procedure which would take about fifteen hours of surgery. And first there was going to be a wedding. Do you Y take IT to be etc etc. Yes of course she does. But they had to be certain Auntie P didn't get wind of the fact that this was no ordinary wedding. If she did, the fat would be well and truly in the fire. Auntie P was conservative in every way, and had even disapproved (strongly) about the heart transplant. Bodies are God-given; you don't shift the pieces around. Auntie P was terribly old, living in practically the mists of time. She had never had any children. History does not of course record whether or not she had a uterus in the first place. Her husband died young in a skiing accident.

There are two main characteristics of Auntie P that have bearing on this story. She was old, as I said, being the great aunt of Y's mother, who was named after her. And she was very very rich (a silver mine and pig farms and chicken farms and a smallgoods factory on the edge of the city). She will die and leave fortunes to deserving relatives. (Oh no – I thought I could just deal with love and maybe death here, but suddenly it all comes down to money.) So Auntie P had to be insulated from the truth, kept in the dark about the transfer of the uterus. Don't let the cat out of the bag. It was easy enough; you tell her lots and lots of good things; you leave out the bad bits. Y is marrying her sweetheart. In church. Happily ever after. End of story.

So Y and IT (and Y's mother of course) had to decide whether to have the wedding before the transplant or the transplant before the wedding. How about having the wedding first, while Y is still in the pink of condition? After all, the surgery, the medication and so forth might (might!) impact on her health and interfere with the beauty of the bride, maybe. They had the wedding. Auntie P was there, and delighted the happy couple with an enormous cheque. We're getting to the bit I don't want to tell you – you might have had an inkling when I used that word 'chunk' back there. Brutal language, used by the surgeons. Yes. Along with the uterus, they had to take *chunks* of blood vessels out of Y's mother, and Y's mother did not survive. She died two weeks after the surgery. Heart attack. Auntie P was too frail to go to the funeral, and was told a few lies about the cause of death. Y was also too fragile to go to her mother's funeral. It was a terrible, conflicted time for everyone. You simply can't imagine the guilt felt by poor Y. The mourning family rallied, and the transplant itself was a great success, Y's mother's uterus living on in Y. The place from which Y came has been placed inside Y and will provide the incubator where Y's child, Y's mother's grandchild, will grow. Everybody seemed to get their head around this without too much trouble.

Y and IT bought a house by the sea, and with energy and hope they set about furnishing a nursery and conceiving a child. The drugs she had to take disagreed with Y, but it was all worth it (apart from the shocking loss of Y's mother) because within due season Y's IVF treatments were successful, and sure enough she was delivered, by caesarean section, of a beautiful baby girl. The child was named Primrose Mary (for such was the full name of not only Auntie P but of Y's mother). She was a living reminder of Y's mother's sacrifice – a rather heavy burden for a little girl. Auntie P sent a very satisfactory cheque and a silver cup for the Baptism (so many religious ceremonies one after another) and also an exquisite set of antique nesting Russian dolls, all royal red and fancy gold. One doll giving birth to another and another and another. Is it remotely possible that somehow Auntie P had got wind of the transplant, and was commenting on it in her own funny old way? Without complaint? Without disapproval? Oh surely not. And yet, and yet, it was an interesting and strangely apposite gift, the Russian dolls. You never quite knew with Auntie P. She had second sight, for one thing. She dreamt about the skiing accident a week before it happened – she tried to stop him from going to the snow, but he *would* go. It would always be a question in the family – how much does Auntie Primrose *know*?

As it turned out, what with the drugs and the IVF and one thing and another, Y and IT decided to have the uterus (it had served its purpose) removed. So Primrose Mary would be their only child. She was healthy and beautiful, and clever as well, bearing many strong resemblances to Y's late mother – although she had her father's eyes. The Russian dolls, arranged in a vermilion row, took pride of place on a high shelf in the nursery – they were admired but never touched. And in the fullness of time little Primrose Mary inherited shares in the silver mine – and became the owner of the smallgoods factory on the edge of the city.

So that's a happy ending, then, isn't it?

DIANE'S FIANCE'S EX-WIFE'S BROTHER'S HEART

I rent an apartment that is not far from the centre of the city. The apartment is on a main highway where trams run in the middle of the road, and two lanes of traffic go on either side of the tracks. We're not far from the zoo, and I have sometimes heard what I take to be the roaring of the lions in the early hours of the morning. Opposite the apartment is a public hospital where the ambulances drive in and out, day and night, day in and day out. Police cars and fire engines drive along the road at high speed, flashing their lights and sounding their sirens. In the sky above the building I often hear helicopters. There's always plenty of noise from outside, and I keep the TV on to counteract it. Sometimes I don't know whether the sirens are on the TV or coming from the world beyond the windows.

Once, Diane from the apartment next door had locked herself out, and so she came in here to wait for her flatmate to get home from work. Diane sat on the sofa watching the News. I was making salad in the kitchen. When the ads came on Diane called out to me to come and look. See that girl advertising skim milk, Diane said, well, she's got a heart transplant. And guess whose heart it is really? I said I couldn't guess. It's my fiancé's ex-wife's brother's heart. I asked her how she knew that, and Diane explained that the brother died in a car accident, and his heart was flown to the hospital across the road by chopper. The same night the girl with the skim milk got a heart. Must be his, Diane said. Because of privacy laws they won't tell you, she said, but I *know* that girl's got the heart. Then Diane started dancing around and singing that song about 'If I give my heart to you' and so forth. She wasn't smiling.

When Diane and her fiancé get married they're going to move out to a house in the suburbs, as far away from here as possible. They're saving up to put a deposit on a house because they just couldn't imagine bringing up children in a place like this. There are several reasons. Diane is actually frightened of the woman in the apartment across the hall. I've tried to tell her the woman is pretty harmless. The woman pins up notices on the door of her place saying things like: 'Abortion is Murder', 'Meat is Murder' and 'Organ Donation is a Sin Against God'.

Diane's fiancé, Alan, is a helicopter pilot, and in December he gets to fly the Santa Clauses around to all the shopping malls and sports' ovals. Alan says that because of the stress that comes with their job, the Santas drink a lot. They get into the helicopter with their sacks full of scotch and vodka and so on, and they make Alan fly round and round in circles while they get up the courage to go on with the job. The drink affects different ones in different ways – some get tearful and sentimental and some get violent. Two of them have fallen asleep in the air, and once one had a mild heart attack and had to be flown to a hospital. Diane told me these things about the Santa Clauses the night she was waiting for her flatmate with the key. By the time Bree got home Diane and I had eaten the salad and some chops and half a frozen cheesecake. While I was grilling the chops the woman from across the hall came over and started banging on the door with a wooden spoon. She always does that. You take no notice, but Diane was freaking out.

Bree sat down and told us about her day in the department store where she works as a Gift Wrapper and also as a Christmas Hamper Consultant. Once she got a special award for selling the most gift items aside from food to go into the hampers. I asked her what sort of things went into hampers and she said everybody, just about, got straightforward things like potted cheeses from England and special honey from the Holy Land and balsamic vinegar from Tasmania. Lots of wine, of course. Then there were amusing things like chocolate-covered ants and pickled cactuses. But it's easy enough, Bree said, to persuade people to include some jewellery and china and glassware and lingerie and linen and perfume. Easy if you know how. One woman spent $1400 on a hamper that she sent to the people she had just bought a house from in a really beautiful area. Diane and I were amazed. Bree told us she heard the story from Kevin in Jams, Jellies and Imported Condiments.

The house had been not just renovated, but completely restored, Kevin said, before the sale. It was almost historic. Not just leadlights and floors and ceiling roses, but whole walls and cellars and things. Chimneys. The garden was to die for, and when the wisteria was in bloom people would get out of their cars to take photos. Once a bride even asked if she could have her wedding pictures taken under the wisteria, and one of those appeared in glossy magazines as an ad for something or other. Now apparently the people who sold the house really loved it, and the woman who bought it actually said over and over again how much she loved it too. They gave her spare tins of paint for touch-ups, and spare slates and pieces of left-over carpet.

But – as soon as the woman had taken possession of the house she had it knocked down so she could build something better. Bree said such things are done these days as a matter of course. And she said it was unusually kind of the woman to send the people the hamper which contained Moët & Chandon, tins of Scottish grouse, as well as chocolate-covered ants, a mystery Norwegian parcel and plenty of other things. Bree said that when she told Mrs Pepper from Lingerie about all this at morning tea, Mrs Pepper said $1400 for knocking down a person's beloved house was nothing these days. She told Bree that people were paying thousands of dollars for nightdresses for their mothers. Diane said if she had sold the house she would have shoved the Moët & Chandon down the buyer's throat. I never thought of Diane as a violent person.

Bree gets a discount on everything she herself buys in the store, and she got a set of stainless steel things such as ice tongs and bottle openers and corkscrews for Diane to give Alan for Christmas. Some of these had dog heads, and some had bird heads. Bree said they were very popular, and she had wrapped up hundreds of them for customers. She had also wrapped six step ladders and one wheelbarrow. She did the ladders up to look like giraffes. Mrs Pepper from Lingerie said she should get a prize for her wrapping.

Then Diane asked Bree if it would be possible to wrap up a helicopter. Diane's idea was that she would arrive at the church on her wedding day in a chopper decorated to resemble a wedding bell. Bree said of course she could do it, but she didn't think it was a very good idea. When Diane asked her why not, Bree admitted that as a matter of fact whenever she saw a chopper going over, it always reminded her of the angel of death. Diane said no, quite the opposite, and just at that minute the girl with the skim milk came back on the TV.

Diane said to take for instance the girl in the ad. If it hadn't been for the helicopter she wouldn't be alive, would she. She wouldn't have been able to get Alan's ex-wife's brother's heart. Bree said she realised all that but she still didn't think a helicopter was the right note for a wedding. Diane said in this case it was perfect, because of Alan's profession. It was like a gesture of respect. They were still arguing about this when they went next door to their apartment.

I think Diane will persuade Bree to wrap up the helicopter, actually. She has the example of the delivery of the Santas on her side, doesn't she? And the argument of the life-giving helicopter with the heart for the girl in the skim milk ad. Her fiancé's ex-wife's brother's heart is kind of a player in all this. These things are hard to ignore.

THE LAWS OF LOVE

FROM PARADISE TO WONDERLAND

I drove past the house yesterday. It's twenty-three years now, twenty-three years since we all left. Well, we left in stages, bit by bit, but it's certainly twenty-three years since I loaded the old Pajero and the camping trailer and headed off. Packed up to the gills. The kids, the dog and the kitchen sink. I can't believe I did it, now that I think back. We ended up in Byron, but we started there, at the house in beautiful Tasmania, with grape vines like a green pattern on a blanket sloping away down the hillside.

We left the dog with my sister Emily in Burnie, and that was just about my one regret. Jake and Skye, poor kids, were heartbroken. They had had Loopy all their lives, but I promised them they could have any pet they wanted when we got where we were going. Where are we going then, mum, they said. And I said we were going to Wonderland. It just came out, and as soon as I'd said it I was sorry. What a dumb thing to say, honestly, but I was desperate I suppose. Skye said the only pet she wanted anyway was Loopy, and she whimpered and blubbered off and on for six days and nearly drove me out of my mind. I wanted Loopy too, but there was no way. Try listening to 'Loooooopy' day in day out in the back of the car, not to mention on the ferry and in every McDonald's and KFC along the highway. But as I say, it only lasted for six days, and then she seemed to get over it.

Jake was mostly silent, thank God, but I know he was mourning for Loopy – well, for a lot of things, actually.

People sometimes say that the destination is not as important as the journey. Well I am here to tell you that sometimes it's the destination that matters, and you can stick the journey up your jumper. Let's just say it was hell and leave it at that. These days the kids remember it fondly, the junk food, the fly-blown motels, the caravan parks, the wind-swept playgrounds full of plastic bags and broken bottles. Weird. But people were kind, you know. I will say that. Although there was the boy that stole Jake's scooter. Yes, there was him. The hardest thing, actually, was keeping our clothes clean. I was forever looking for laundromats and trying to collect enough coins. And everything came out grey anyway. Mum, Skye would say, mum, when do we get to Wonderland? It's a long way, I would say, a long way. But we'll get there in the end, baby. And we did.

My friend Gretel was living in Byron with her man of the time. That was Snoddy. She was making bead jewellery and selling it in markets, and Snods was doing huge paintings – mainly tropical flowers – frangipani and hibiscus and so on. Such things were popular at the time with big banks and hotels in the cities, and they were hung on vast marble walls. Snoddy used to sing 'I dreamt I dwelt in marble halls.' I still see the paintings sometimes, in the odd bank and so forth. I always thought they were hideous, and I still do, but they certainly paid the bills.

So we settled down with Gretel and Snoddy and their various kids. Jake and Skye fitted right in, and I got a job in a wine bar, cleaning and also serving drinks. This is the life, eh Tabbycat, Snoddy would say to me. Aren't you glad you make the effort? And I was. I put the terrible journey north – it went on forever

– behind me, and got into the swing of things in Byron. I got into crystals and Tarot easy as, and into a bit of massage. Snoddy built me a wigwam and I operated from there. One day Skye said to me – I remember this as if it was yesterday – she said, Wonderland is wonderful, mum. You were right to come here. I love it. And then she hugged me and she said, I love you forever, mum. We wore flowers in our hair, and the atmosphere was sweet with patchouli and cannabis. The kids went to school in bare feet. Yes, they took to it all like ducks to water. Jake learnt to play the bongos, and Skye began the dancing that finally took her to New York. So this was Wonderland.

As I drove by the house on the hill yesterday, it was hard to believe I had done what I had done, broken from my life there at the vineyard. Escaped. I can go over it all in my mind now without really feeling the horror and the fear – horror and chaos every day, fear of the future. The legal battles were to come, as I drove off with the kids from that failed Paradise on the hill.

I suppose it all started when I fell in love with Salv. Yes. And we had a double wedding with his brother Fabio. Wedding bells like that should ring alarm bells, in retrospect. The brothers bought the vineyard and started to build the house on the hill – the famous double house where two families would live together with one fabulous swimming pool and stables for horses – and a vast garage splitting the house in two. That word 'splitting'. Always watch out for splitting.

Fabio married Anka – Anka with the shining golden hair and wide dreaming aquamarine eyes. She was the great beauty of the district. We were a lovely mixture of Italian, Anglo and Polish. Watch out for 'mixture' too. That's another word.

Mixture and splitting and alarm bells. Yes. Anka's family were Holocaust survivors – her mother was one of the babies smuggled out of Poland in a big leather handbag. I thought her married name – Anka Foglieri – was really pretty, whereas mine – Tabitha Foglieri – was kind of a mouthful. Mixture. My mother – as Anglo as they come, and they came pretty Anglo in Tassie in the sixties – believed that the world should somehow resemble the world of Beatrix Potter, and yes, I was named after Tabitha Twitchit, the mother cat in the apron. Everybody used to give me figurines of her – I faithfully collected them for years. In fact I hated them. When I left the vineyard, they stayed behind in the shadow box on the wall of Skye's old bedroom. I've sometimes wondered what became of them. They might be worth a fortune now. Too bad.

Things went well for a few years. We were the envy of the district with a flourishing vineyard and wine label 'Tabianka Cellars', and our great mansion on the hill. The Foglieri Castle – that's what people called it, the Foglieri Castle. Foglieri Folly more like.

I don't know when the rows started, but the rot set in, and while the vines flourished, the lives of us two families in the castle started to go to hell. Gretel said she saw it coming long before I did – well she had her crystal ball up there in Byron. Salv fell in love with Anka, didn't he. I think, to her credit, that she resisted him for a long time, but in the end Fabio caught them in the cabana and went after Salvatore with a shotgun. He never explained why he was carrying the gun at the time. No – that was never explained. Anyhow, he threatened, didn't pull the trigger, but it was going to be only a matter of time. The stress of it all actually killed my mother, I reckon. We tried to sort things out – counsellors and priests and lawyers, not to mention the families and friends, but it went from bad to worse and in the end I packed the Pajero and got out. I hardly even planned it. The big casualty at that point was Loopy, but actually he lived a long and happy life with Emily and Tom and their kids. We got another golden lab before too long in Byron, so everyone was happy. Well that sounds kind of neat. Nothing was neat, really, was it, not with everything simmering away at the Foglieri Folly. Simmering? More like doing whatever it is volcanoes do. Salvatore's dad originally came from Naples, and whenever he got into a temper the family used to call him Vesuvius. Well Vesuvius was about to blow.

While we were settling, or drifting down in Wonderland, there was trouble, naturally, back in Paradise. Big trouble. Fabio did eventually go after Salvatore with the shotgun. He killed him down among the vines very early one crisp morning in spring. 'Let us get up early to the vineyard' – that's from the Bible. Then he went up to the house and had a swim. Yes. He was still in the pool when the police came. So Fabio went to jail. Simple. Anka had a complete breakdown. It all worked out like an equation. I had to go back of course, but when it was all over, Salvatore's funeral and the trial and so forth, I returned to Byron for good.

It seems strange to tell these terrible facts so bluntly, but they have kind of solidified in my mind, and I trot them out like an old legend or something. My children have no father any more. I have never really spoken to Anka since I left, all those years ago. Of course we've had plenty of legal dealings – we sold the house – and we see each other at funerals. I must say she looks very beautiful in black, with lace obscuring her face and her aquamarine eyes gazing sorrowfully out. I do feel sorry for her, yes, I do.

Some people from France, actually, bought the house and the business, and they didn't change the label because it has been so successful, particularly overseas. So there they are in grog shops all over the world, sparkling glass bottles with a picture of the house on the hill and the vines plaiting their way down the hillside in the sunlight, and the word 'Tabianka' scrawled in thick blue handwriting across the middle. Gretel laughs a kind of dark laugh and calls it one of the ironies of the gods. And more ironic is the fact that we can't usually afford to drink anything as expensive as Tabianka, even though we're doing well. Sometimes we do lash out and have a bottle of Tabianka, though. I thought it would choke me, but it's so smooth and rich that even I'm completely seduced.

Snoddy eventually went off to live in Perth with a young woman who worked, as it happened, for a bank where they had one of his big flower paintings – it was a waterlily one – nothing like Monet. He dreamt he dwelt in marble halls. So that left Gretel and me and five kids. The kids have more or less gone now, and that leaves Gretel and me. We have a pretty good business providing massage and aromatherapy to all the big hotels in Byron and points north. My old wigwam is still there out in the yard.

Well, the drive past the house on the hill, with its sloping carpet of vines, brought it all back to me. It's all behind me now. Listen to your heart, Gretel used to say – she still does. I listened then and I listen now, and the answer is not difficult to hear. Of course then you have to have the strength to follow your heart, don't you? That was the hard part – remember Loopy and the laundromats and the broken bottles in the playgrounds. But now there's Gretel and me, at home in Wonderland.

Whatever next, I say, whatever next, and Gretel smiles her enigmatic smile and holds me in her arms and says whatever will be will be.

And I suppose it will.

HIGHWAY TO HEAVEN

The San Francisco artist Josu Otxoa began his series of 'Highway to Heaven' paintings in the early 1970s when he was newly arrived from South America. The series grew to be a vast hyper-real collection of canvases in bold colours, depicting the highways of the US in all their mysterious detail and danger, bleak and gaudy and full of dark and shining promise. Desert-mountain-city-sea, straight and winding. The signs the billboards the motels the gas stations the lights the trailers the cars the cars the cars. Dust, smog, rain, hail, shine. These pictures are the icons of the hitch-hiker's religious brotherhood. They tell the story of the eternal traveller who puts his faith in The Road. Nothing but The Road. The Road is God and King and Everyman and Everything. The Road is the Highway to Salvation, the Highway to Heaven.

In every picture there appears – sometimes dominant, sometimes minuscule, a mere manufacturer's logo, an insect – the figure of a young blonde woman in a black and white polka dot dress. Petticoat milky underneath, skirt billowing. The artist called her 'Annette'. When Otxoa died in 2008, he was seventy-five, the series was still, according to his calculations, incomplete.

After the artist's death his widow, American poet Lauren Tharp set about the task of assembling the 'Highway to Heaven' show for exhibition. There was one long work in sections – the road would stretch around a room – and in this one there were in fact five images, different sizes, different angles, of Annette. The little figure even appeared as a cheerful angel drifting out from behind a looming slate-grey cloud.

People asked who Annette might be, and it had long since become accepted that she was, as Josu used to say with a shrug, a figment of the imagination, everybody's girl, everyman's companion on life's journey. This was, of course, part artist's bullshit, and Lauren didn't really take much interest in who Annette might or might not be.

But now that you have the artist dead, and the artist's wife sorting through studio and attic and cellar, you will have realised that there might be an impending revelation. In the normal course of such events, in a tattered grey folder of scrappy papers and meaningless ephemera, Lauren finds a small manila envelope which contains two faded colour photographs. One is the picture of a pretty young blonde in a black and white polka dot dress with a billowing skirt and a visible puff of creamy petticoat. She is posing, laughing, beside the fountain of the lions in the Alhambra. The date on the back of the photograph is 1965. The other picture is also of Annette, this time accompanied by a tall handsome youthful grinning Josu. They are standing, arms entwined, outside the Prado.

To a wife like Lauren, or perhaps to almost any wife, these pictures are really no surprise. And what does it matter who Annette was or is or what she meant to the artist Josu, now deceased? But you know and I know how such sudden manifestations of past matters can flash up on a widow's recent mind and can begin to shimmer in the dark bub-bub bub-bub of a widow's recent heart. Not that Lauren went looking on *purpose* for the story behind the pictures, not that she set out to find documents, letters, diaries, notes. But in the normal course of sorting-out events she did find them – well, she found a diary. And what the diary told her did in fact explain, if such explanation were needed, and perhaps it was and perhaps it wasn't, that the inspiration for the life-long project-obsession 'Highway to Heaven' was to be found in the events of the spring of 1965 on the roads and byways of Spain.

Lauren herself met Josu in Madrid in the summer of 1965. So you see she was probably right to feel a certain sense of betrayal as the revelation unfolded. I think it is fair enough to say it 'unfolded' since Lauren opened the grey folder, opened the manila envelope, and later from the deep recess of a cabin trunk opened up a soft black notebook which turned out to be The Diary.

Lauren had been an American girl working her way round Europe. She was going door to door selling toothpaste. Please believe me, this is true. And she knocked on an apartment door which was opened by the tall, young, handsome and oh so sad Josu whose beloved Irish rose Annette had recently run away, literally run away into the twilight never to be seen again. Josu rallied quickly, bought all the toothpaste, and swiftly, oh so swiftly, before you could even clap a castanet or light a candle to your best and favourite saint, he and Lauren were on their way to a new life in California, via Mexico, where they eventually became 'man and wife', painter and poet, both mildly celebrated for their works.

What Lauren learnt from the diary put many funny little details into place, and the diary told her that Annette had known one man, whereas Lauren had really married someone else. Was the second Josu a fraud? Or was the first one, perhaps the fake. Where was the real masquerade? It seemed to Lauren, in the long run, that her man was the real one, and that the painter with his angel on the Highway to Heaven was himself a confection, a kind of sprite.

According to the diary, the affair between Josu and Annette was a short three-week thing that happened at a time when Josu was at a terrible turning point or crossroad in his life. Virtually all of the details of his life-before-Lauren were new to Lauren as she read of them, in 2008. It turned out Josu had been brought up in a little industrial town in the Basque country of northern Spain. (Lauren did know this, but had believed that virtually the whole family had one way or another died out, what with time, and age, and disease – separatism, terrorism etc.) He had entered a seminary at the age of seven, and by the age of twenty-five he was a priest. He spoke five languages with great fluency, and spent a year at a parish in London. According to the diary, if the diary is to be believed, in London he gave more time to whores than he did to his devotions or his responsibilities. He also 'fell in love' with a lot of girls – in the street, on the Tube, in shops and also in Museums and parks and gardens.

He returned to Spain and was sent to a small dark parish (he always wrote this in the diary, which was in English, as 'perish' – he liked a joke) in the wilds of the Basque country. Perhaps the idea was that he would forget everything he had seen and done in London, that he would reform. Who knows? In any case what happened was that in the depths of one dark Basque night he spirited himself up and away and out of his small dark perish and got himself (yes, he was hitch-hiking) as far as Burgos where he went into hiding in the house of an artist he met in a bar. The freedom and the anonymity and the dislocation and the danger and the instant rapport he felt as he rode in the cars of strangers became beautifully addictive. He could be anybody. He told marvellous lies. He was in fact on the first stage of his own personal Highway to Heaven. This was his purpose, his meaning, his high. He had become an outlaw. Drivers would always pick up a man in priest's uniform, and he was such a man. The danger in this was outweighed by the need to get the ride. He got the ride. And somehow he was protected from being discovered by the Church and the Law. He had a habit of invoking St Christopher out loud in his lovely voice, and perhaps this worked.

For the Church was hunting him. The Law was seeking him. He, King of the Highway, would evade them. They got close to catching him in Burgos, so he set off for Madrid. He headed for a church where he knew there was strong sympathy for Basque separatists. Not that he could in fact care less about Basque separatists. But, wearing his priestly collar and tucking his black leather brief-case under his arm, he fronted up to the door and spun a story about collecting money for The Cause. He was working in secret he told the priest, and so he was given shelter and food and funds.

And one day, while strolling in the Retiro Park, he met the clever pretty little Irish girl, Annette, in her black and white polka dot etc etc. He realised she was everything he had ever wanted, and that very afternoon they lay, lovers among the shrubbery of the Retiro Park. How dangerous was that! But so thrilling. Annette was a dancer hoping to get work in Madrid.

'Oh – come with me to Mexico instead. We are meant to be together,' he says.

'OK,' she says, 'but first I would really like to go to Granada because I want to see the Alhambra. It's very lucky. The fountain of the lions is very lucky.'

'How so?'

'My mother said. She went there and made a wish and she won a whole lot of money the next day.'

This sounded like a very good idea to him.

'OK. We'll hitch-hike to Granada.'

'I thought we could go on the train.'

The train, however, was too dangerous for him, full of Civil Guard in shiny black hats, and Church spies in long grey overcoats. Not possible. You need papers on the train. On the road – no papers needed. The freedom of the road.

'Hitch-hiking is best. It's so much fun and cheaper. And think of the people you meet.'

'I have thought about them. I don't particularly want to meet them.'

Well, a little more of his blarney and a lot more of his lovemaking (this time in her room which was in fact in a convent, her aunt was a nun, for heaven's sake) and they were on the road to Granada, each with a tiny canvas bag of possessions. He explained to her that he was running from the Church and from the Law, and this appealed to her dancing Irish heart. The best plan, he said, was for him to put on this clerical collar and stop the cars, and then he would produce her and explain that she was his student from Ireland. No cars would stop for a woman, but all cars would stop for a priest. This proved to be the case.

Because of the problem of his papers, they could never stay in hotels. So he would talk his way into the hearts of priests at their church doors, and a bed would be found for him, and a bed for Annette would be found with a good woman of whom there appeared to be many. Sometimes, and this is rather shocking, he would be offered the chance by the priest to say the Mass that day in the church, and of course he would do so. Annette found this almost too much to bear, too great a transgression of too many laws. She knew that a dark Irish punishment awaited both of them if they went on like this. Hell, she supposed.

They made it to the Alhambra, and he took the fountain picture with Annette's little camera, and an American man who had taken a shine to Annette took the picture of the pair of them – the Spanish priest and his Irish student. When the pictures were printed Annette gave both of them to Josu. They now lay loosely, faded, in the diary.

The diary tells the story from the point of view of Josu, of course. But as she read it Lauren could imagine how Annette began to feel the pull of reality against the fantasies of her handsome lover's will. Annette keeps wanting to return to Madrid by train; Josu will never hear of this. He has begun to speak of the roads as their 'Highway to Heaven'. He seems to think that they can somehow hitch-hike their way to Mexico.

'I have a friend in Cadiz – he has a boat – he will take us to Mexico. We will have new papers.'

But Annette, unlike Josu, has not cut loose from her family in county Sligo. She sends postcards to her mother and her sisters and her girlfriends. This affair is to her a three-week interlude on the road; to Josu it seems to be, or he hopes and imagines it is, the beginning of a new life in the new world.

They argued. They hitch-hiked. They were heading north.

It was twilight in Madrid. The old black car driven by a professor of philosophy from the University of Madrid stopped at a busy intersection and, just as they were about to move forward, suddenly Annette, who had been plotting and planning, her canvas bag tight in her fist, leapt out the door and seemed to dissolve into a knot of trees. (The door flew open, she shot out, dissolved into a knot of trees as the car moved on. The door slammed itself shut. I called to the driver to stop but this was not possible. I tried to get out and chase her but my door was stuck. It was over. She was gone. 'She will come back,' said the professor wisely and sadly. I knew she was gone forever. I knew this in my heart. My heart was broken, forever.)

The date of this entry was four days before Lauren arrived with the toothpaste.

So that was it. Exit Annette. Enter Lauren. And so began the whole new life of Josu Otxoa the San Francisco painter whose series 'Highway to Heaven' is now about to be hailed as one of the greatest American road series in the history of road series.

And people say to Lauren: 'So who was that girl then?'

And Lauren says: 'Oh a figment – just a figment of his imagination.'

MY BELOVED IS MINE AND I AM HIS

Seventeen children squint into the Australian sun, and they are fixed there forever in the doorway of the country school. Big boys and girls of thirteen and fourteen down to little ones of six. Most of the children look strong and healthy, hopeful, quizzical, innocent. All are trying their best to please the photographer, their teacher Mr Anthony, trying to hold still, to smile, to obey. The part-time assistant Miss Fitzpatrick has shepherded the children into lines, bunched them up outside the battered double doors, told them to straighten their clothes, hold still. It is a black and white picture.

Now is the end of the year — for some it is the end of an era — the beginning of the Christmas holidays. Long hot lazy days under the gums and willows beside the winding river. Visits from cousins, visits to grandparents, presents in red cellophane, crinkly — crêpe paper chains across the mantelpiece, pudding (steamy, spicy, filled with boiled money, swimming in cream) roast goose, gravy, cherries, lemonade. All this information crams itself into the photograph as church services and Christmas carols and gleaming brass vases filled with waving poppies and soft red gum tips quiver just outside the frame. So beautiful, Silent Night, Holy Night. Santa Claus and sprigs of holly bejewelled with gleaming scarlet berries.

Standing in the back row, happily leaning together, obediently smiling and squinting into the light are Moira and Patricia. Moira's head is slightly tilted to the side; Patricia looks straight into the camera, trusting, steady brown eyes under a severe brown fringe of hair. These two good friends will enjoy the bright days by the snaking river, stretched out in the sun, swimming, laughing, riding bikes, playing tennis. But they know, in the photograph, that at the end of the summer everything will change. Yes, it is the end of an era. You can read all this in their faces, fixed forever in black and white and shades of grey.

Moira will stay on the farm and go by bus every day to the Academy of Mary Immaculate. But Patricia, the cleverest girl in the group, has won a scholarship to a Church of England school far far away in a large country town. She will live at the church hostel and go to school with girls from all over the place. Scary but exciting.

As they all squint into the light of the future, the shutter clicks. The photograph is captive in the small black box. Mr Anthony laughs and Miss Fitzpatrick claps her hands and the seventeen children scatter, most of them scurrying into the shade of the pepper trees. Patricia stays a quiet moment to say goodbye and thank you. Mr Anthony and Miss Fitzpatrick smile, and nod goodbye and good luck.

The little ones took home their paintings, the big boys took their woodwork – pencil cases and crumb trays. Donald Murfett made a jewel-box for his mother. The big girls took their embroidery, coarse white stitching on scarlet linen squares. Moira won the embroidery prize, her work the image of a butterfly with the text: 'All Things Bright and Beautiful'. Patricia had embroidered a spindly scorpion with the words: 'You cannot hurt anybody without receiving greater hurt.' Miss Fitzpatrick had tried to talk her out of it – what about a nice kitten?

Mr Anthony pressed into Patricia's hand a book, a copy of the poems of Robert Browning, a goodbye gift. Patricia was surprised and a little embarrassed and bewildered.

Later she thanked him in a Christmas card, a picture of young people in long dark coats and fur caps and muffs skating on blue ice.

To the surprise of many, Miss Fitzpatrick and Mr Anthony were married in late January. The whole school went to the wedding in the white wooden Catholic church which was decorated with dreaming white arum lilies, clouds of pink roses, and green crêpe paper. Four small girls solemn in green and pink, and the priest stiff and gleaming in cream and gold, all edged in fine glittering scarlet, bowing and muttering in the sing-song salvation melodies of Latin. Bernadette Mary in yards of icy lace took Edward James in his dark brown suit and deep dark burgundy tie to be her lawful wedded husband, and Patricia and Moira wept tears of wonder and excitement and joy. Moira's mother played the organ, Sylvia Daniels with her wild red hair flaming and flying all over everywhere sang 'Ave Maria'. Glorious. The congregation sang 'Where there is charity and love, there the God of love abides.' Confetti from here to kingdom come, and wagging tongues wittered and wiggled about the state of Bernadette's waistline, but nothing ever came of it. She had twins two years later, and other babies down the track.

At home was Patricia's small bedroom at the back of the house, the bedroom she shared with her much older sister until Shirley went to Sydney to study to be a stenographer. The room was dark, set underneath the shadowy dusty row of pine trees. Patricia stretched out on the bed, lying on the quilt her granny made long long ago, and tried to think of the future. Her own future. All her very own. She could not imagine it. The poems of Browning in their green suede cover lay on the chest of drawers beside her bed, the red and white scorpion was still in her schoolbag. She ran the palms of her hands across the lovely rough woolly surface of the quilt – it was what is known as a 'wagga', a patchwork of knitted woollen scraps, with a filling of old woollen clothing, heavy and cosy and so comforting, smelling of home and the past and sweet dark nights. The colours were muted, greens and purples and browns, stitched together by candlelight with love.

Can I take Wagga with me to Hightower – she asked her mother – please? But her mother said no, people would not understand. You have to learn to fit in with the others.

But I love him, truly. Why can't I take him with me? I have always had Wagga, ever since I can remember. Why can't I though? He's mine anyhow. Wagga is mine.

Her mother sighed. Patricia was such a child in many ways.

Because – because people would make fun of you, Patricia. You have to think of that you know. And there will be blankets at the hostel. Regulation. They will be regulation.

Patricia's eyes filled for a moment with tears, but then she looked away. When her gaze came back to her mother it was steady brown again, perhaps even a little harder.

<u>*Moira Looks at the Photograph – 2003*</u>
Moira, a respectable widow and grandmother and retired member of the Shire Council, Vice-President of the Regional Catholic Family Society, winner more than once of the landscape painting section of the Art Club, searched through her photo albums until she came to the picture Mr Anthony took at

the end of 1953. The year before Patricia went off to Hightower. It was strange, and sad, Moira always thought, the way Patricia wrote her one letter from her new school – and then nothing. Blank. She did not answer Moira's letters after that, and before very long Moira stopped writing. In the holidays Moira brought home new friends, and she hardly ever saw Patricia. When Patricia came home in disgrace after nearly three years, the bond was broken. Moira's family didn't want her to have anything to do with Patricia any more. Christian charity was one thing, but mixing with a bad type of girl was quite another. Patricia had been caught with boys and expelled from Hightower, so she was no longer fit company for a nice girl. Moira courted Vincent Hazelwood from the general store, and eventually they married. Things had worked out for Moira; they had not worked out for Patricia.

Patricia's father died. Her mother went to live with relatives in South Australia. Patricia went to Sydney, did part of the training for nursing, married Kevin Shelby who used to beat her up, had three children, separated from Kevin who later drank himself to death. Where did that leave Patricia? Heaven knows.

Moira had the school picture on the table when Patricia arrived for the visit. Moira did not know what to expect, did not know why Patricia wanted to see her after all these years. She felt quite awkward. There was a great poignancy to the photo, its grey tones just as crisp and telling – more telling in fact – as they had been all that long time ago. Moira remembered Mr Anthony, Miss Fitzpatrick, the way they fussed about getting everyone to stand up tight against each other in the doorway.

I need to talk to somebody, Moira – Patricia said. I have never had anybody to talk to. Ever, really. I have bottled everything up, for all these years, and I can't think of anybody I can trust. Except I thought of you. One night, one night I thought of you, and now I hope I can come and see you, perhaps, and I can talk to you, and you will listen. Could it be that Patricia was ill, terminally ill, dying, lost and lonely and dying? That was the only thing Moira could think of really, that Patricia must be ill and frightened and lonely and in need of an old, old friend. Where there is charity and love.

The steady brown eyes, a hint of tears, under the same fringe, but grey. The voice was firm and sweet, the same voice. There was something eerie about that voice.

I thought I could talk to you, she said, I thought I could talk to you, Moira, and you would listen and you would understand.

What Moira Might Say

The photo is fifty years old. All that time. Can that be right? Fifty years! Fifty years and when she wanted somebody to talk to, Patricia thought of me. Over the years I have sometimes thought of her, I have even imagined, sometimes, talking to her. About this and that. But now it was not going to be this and that, I could tell. Something was very serious, and the past was coming back, coming out of its silent shadow-cupboard – what do they say – skeletons in the cupboard? She rang out of the blue, right out of the blue, and I knew her voice straight away, just like I knew her walk. I looked out the lounge room window and I saw her at the gate. She stopped for a second as if she was getting her breath, or getting up her courage, or adjusting her mind – or something – and then she kind of swung through the gate the way she used to, almost, and came slowly but purposefully up the path. It is quite a distance from the gate to the front porch, and the path, yellow concrete, twists and turns – Vin's father put that path in probably sixty years ago now, more probably, and it isn't even hardly cracked. After all this time. Patricia slowed down as she got closer, she seemed to peer down every now and then as if she wanted to look at the petunias. I am proud of the petunias this year, huge pink and purple ones, and all blooming at once. Huge. I love petunias. I seem to remember that Patricia used to like them too. Or does my memory play tricks on me? She was wearing a green overcoat, olive green, straight with no waist, and time was stopped or you might say suspended for a while so I could look at Patricia in her old-fashioned overcoat, moving along the yellow winding path. Towards me. I was standing at the window watching her, considering. She looked, I thought, somehow *beautiful* in the overcoat, making her steady silent way towards me. The world was silent and standing still, as Patricia, wearing a coat that reminded me of – her mother – came drifting, that's what it was, drifting like in a dream, up the front path to the door. She looked thinner than I had expected, and her neat black shoes were very soft and fashionable. Elegant. Elegant shoes and good stockings. A large brown shoulder bag, saggy and comfortable, worn, trustworthy. It was Patricia. She came up onto the porch and I lost sight of her. The bell rang, deengle-dongle-deee and I found I could not bring myself to move from the window. I looked out onto the path, looked at the petunias all huge and pink and purple, soft and frilly in the sunlight beside the path, and the path was empty, and Patricia was at the door, waiting innocently for me to open it for her. I took a few deep breaths – I was nervous after all these years – and then I went out into the hall and opened the door. Hello. Patricia.

Patricia and Moira Meet for the First Time in Fifty Years

The bell has rung and Patricia steps back from the welcome mat which has a design of red roses wreathed around the edge. It seems wrong to stand on those roses. Her shoulders are held proudly back, yet her face is deeply suffused with sorrow, pain, anguish, memories of hurt. Every single step that has brought her to this doorway is present in her memory as she stands there, every moment present in sharp detail and relief.

Some memories are like hallucinations.

She remembers the day her mother and father left her at the hostel and Mrs Cutler came forward smiling and held out her hands in welcome, and took her up the stairs to the dormitory where the narrow beds were covered with their regulation blankets and their regulation brown and orange and green striped counterpanes, squared at the corners and rubbed thin in places. Then her mother and father had dissolved, her mother's blue straw hat, small and neat with darker blue flowers, her father's gabardine overcoat and tartan scarf, smelling of pipe tobacco — gone. Her mother's hands moved lightly across Patricia's face, and then they were gone. Gone forever. The other girls came, and they all put their things into the drawers and wardrobes, shyly, slyly looking at each other out of the corners of their eyes. There were eight girls at the hostel, others boarded at the school.

Mrs Cutler was so bright and friendly, the long fluff of her pink bunnywool bolero fuzzing around her in a softly moving halo, and so jolly, and soon it was time to go down to afternoon tea and guess who was waiting there in the big study beside the fireplace – Father Cutler himself! Lawrence Cutler beaming and throwing out his arms and crying: 'Welcome, girls, welcome to our home! Lorraine and I will be your hosts, and you will be our guests! May we all enjoy health and happiness and do lots and lots of homework!' There was laughter and his voice was full of exclamation marks. He stood by the fireplace, there were lazy electric logs glowing eerily in the hearth, and Father Cutler shone, he shone in the firelight and he shone from within. No heat came from the fire, but in the winter heat would be turned on. Father Cutler was a gleaming, glowing, shining, lightning rod of joy and welcome and goodness. The two tiny Cutler girls, Georgina and Annabelle, in pastel smocked dresses, stood quietly and obediently by their mother, sucking their thumbs. Scones and blackberry jam and cream and raspberry cordial. You may call me Mother Lorraine, said Mrs Cutler. Then a prayer of hope and blessing, and a new life had begun.

This was the last thing Patricia had expected, this cosy family affair of scones and cream beside the flickering lifeless fire.

She remembers the church services and the sound of Father Cutler's voice, a voice like a storyteller of ancient times, a voice like an angel or a prophet. The girls would flock around him in the stone archway after the Eucharist, and he would laugh and joke and be there, firmly on the gravel path, in loco parentis. There were classes in church doctrine where the girls were taught in a group, sitting around on the leather sofa, on the tapestry armchairs, on the skin rug on the floor before the fire.

Is this a fox skin rug, Father Cutler?

It is, actually.

Oh, it's lovely.

In fact I shot the critters myself. Had them made into a rug.

It's a lot of foxes!

Yes, yes it is a lot of foxes.

And Father Cutler glows by the red and purple logs, smiles and beams and talks softly and thoughtfully. The eyes of all the girls around him tell him he is already beloved – he is good, kind, adored, believed, trusted. And Lorraine brings in milk and shortbread and stays to join in the fun of Doctrine and Scripture. They all love to discuss miracles – loaves and fishes as well as other quite Catholic-sounding stories about rose petals and apparitions. They have Confirmation Classes, are being prepared to wear white dresses and veils and receive the Holy Ghost when Bishop Stonycroft comes. The young Bishop and his wife are celebrities, he a tall imposing smooth-talking confident man in his towering mitre and billowing cope, she a small twittering moth of a woman in brilliant pinks and peacock blues, silk from Thailand, and with an astonishing array of perky and elaborate hats covered in flowers and feathers and sequins and curly rolls of fine straw. The episcopal couple whirl through the town, the school, the hostel, the church. Everyone feels very honoured, especially the young people who receive the gift of the Holy Ghost. May He guide and comfort you always. Bishop Stonycroft performs the Laying on of Hands.

Father is a great believer in having incense and lots of candles burning in the church, and he hears the Confessions of his flock who all honour, trust and adore him. He would take the girls in pairs up to the top of the bushfire lookout tower – no it is not dangerous ladies – and show them the vast sweep of the landscape, out out to the end of nowhere, one hand on the shoulder of each girl.

Look at that, ladies. Look at God's gorgeous world. And he would recite some verses by Gerard Manley Hopkins. 'I caught this morning morning's minion.'

Patricia remembers also the individual tutorials each girl had with Father Cutler. She felt so important sitting there beside him deep in the leather undulations of the sofa, brown and warm. In the evening, parchment lampshades cast a holy-scholarly glow on the books they read. Poetry books and the Bible.

'My beloved is mine and I am his, he feedeth among the lilies.'

You love the *Song of Solomon* don't you Patricia?

Yes Father.

'Set me as a seal upon thine heart' – beautiful, is it not?

And when Patricia said in a soft and nervous voice that yes it was beautiful, Father Cutler put his own beautiful hand, the hand that blessed the bread and wine, the hand that would one day slip the Body of Christ between her lips at the Communion rail, the hand that buttered scones and passed them one by one and bit by bit into her mouth, he put his hand on her hand, very lightly, and he smiled his halo smile and he looked into her eyes. She knew she was his favourite, his very own chosen acolyte and favourite. There was a deep and spiritual secrecy about this fact. It made her warm and delicious deep inside.

And time went on, and life in the hostel became more and more sweet and beautiful. One evening early – it was a soft and yellow twilight – as Father and Patricia were sitting on the sofa discussing the life of Saint Elizabeth and placing the petals of a rose in pale pink patterns on the low table, Father took both her hands in his and he placed his face very close to hers and looked deep down into her eyes so that he was looking into her heart, and he said:

You know that Lorraine is a good woman, don't you?

Patricia was surprised. Yes, I know.

She is like a mother to all you girls, and she does her very best to be a good wife to me.

There was a sizzling silence in the study. Patricia found it hard to know what she was supposed to say. She said nothing.

Yes, she does her best, but the truth is, Pittie-Pat, the truth is that Lorraine does not in fact fulfil my needs.

The silence sizzles on.

She has asked me to ask you if you would do some things for me, to help her, if you understand.

Lawrence Cutler was quite certain the plain fourteen-year-old girl from her little country town did not understand. Her steady silence told him that, but he continued.

We must lock the study door now, see, I am locking the study door, and we are going to have a small glass of wine, and I am going to play some quiet and delightful music. Listen to the harp and to the little flutes, listen.

As the music wove its delicate spell, and the wine began to work its warmth in Patricia's blood, Lawrence gently removed her tie, her shirt, his tie, his shirt, her skirt, his trousers, their underwear, until they stood by the fire in their socks, his black, hers white, and he lifted her up, his body was astonishing-white and muscular-lovely, and he placed her on the wild surface of the tawny fox skin rug, and he kissed her and fondled her and when she was moist and pink and open, he slowly – and this was delicious – he whispered to her that he had been sent not only by Lorraine but also by God to teach her how to reach a state of spiritual ecstasy. So with those holy hands, beautiful hands from the altar, hands that blessed brides and babies and also blessed dead people, he stroked her and rocked her until she was filled with sudden warmth and light and music. And then he moved himself inside her, and they were One, he said they were One, on the fox skin rug in the study in the late twilight.

He removed their socks and flung them across the room with a laugh.

Foxes in soxes and this little piggy went to market.

You are perfect, and filled with the love of God, and I love you with all my heart, Pittie-Pat. This is of course our finest sacred secret, never to be shared. Stand up now. Wiggle your toes into the fur of the naughty naughty little foxes. Foxes in soxes. Do you want to see my hunting rifle? I can show it to you if you like.

He giggled.

And she stood and nodded, breathless with her own ecstasy of initiation, her breasts hot and hard again in his hands as he stood again behind her and pushed into her again. There was a little blood which Lawrence wiped away with his own white linen handkerchief. Then he kissed the handkerchief. And then he burnt it in the flame of a candle, letting the ash fall onto the deep russet surface of the fox skin rug. He smiled. From a slender cupboard beside the fireplace the priest took his hunting rifle. Such things were not strange to Patricia. She was a country girl. But the naked man with the rifle which he pointed at her in jest – that was strange. Strange and thrilling too.

It became a ritual – the love-making on the fox skin rug and then the revelation of the rifle in the cupboard, like a warning to little foxes.

One day we will truly be together and I will marry you and you will have my child and we will live in Paradise. Lorraine is very pleased with how things are going, and she has agreed. It is even possible that you will have a child quite soon – that would be wonderful. I sense that I have put into you the spirit of our child.

What would happen about school?

They will be completely understanding. Paradise is the realm of the blessed. Your belly is as a sheaf of wheat.

In fact Lawrence was careful to protect the sheaf of wheat from any danger of fertilisation, but Patricia did not realise this. In church Lawrence wore the most shimmering and elaborate vestments, moved beneath the stiff embroidered chasubles like a magnificent chess-piece on secret wheels. Sometimes he wore a grey suit and his collar, and other times he wore a swinging black cassock with a leather belt, like a fantastic medieval monk. He always stood out in a crowd.

During the holidays when Patricia went home to her parents she began receiving letters in square cream envelopes, letters written in powerful square black handwriting, letters from Lawrence. She would collect the family mail from the post office herself, vigilant and helpful. The walk to the post office was filled with breathless anticipation; the walk home a slow and blissful pilgrimage to the shrine in her bedroom where she kept a photograph, so innocent, of herself and three other girls on the steps of the hostel with Father Cutler. She kept the letters in an old leather bag, in the hollow of the pine tree outside her bedroom window. Dust and insects and spiders could get in, but the eyes that pry out secrets never gazed upon the Letters that Lawrence Wrote to Patricia.

Dear Patricia, I miss you very much. My own dearest love, I long to hold you in my arms, to feel your sweet soft breasts against my body. I long to lie with you, to lie all night long beside the Shalimar, Your longing, loving, lost and wandering Lawrence. Write to me. I must hear that you are true to me. I drink your juices. Loving sacred kisses, kisses all over your peaches and cream. We will

*make a holy child together, and we will walk together
forever in the fields of Almighty God.*

Patricia did not, as it happened, conceive a child. The one who
conceived was Lorraine, and Patricia was shocked. She had
done the work and now Lorraine was getting all the attention,
getting fat.

Mrs Cutler's expecting! Look at her stomach! The girls
whispered to each other in excited fascination. Imagine Father
and Mrs Cutler doing that and getting another baby.

The visits to the study stopped. Suddenly. And one Sunday
Father preached a sermon about how God moves in mysterious
ways, and how our hopes and dreams and prayers are sometimes
answered in ways that we could not have expected. Patricia
wept. She could no longer eat. Her school work suffered. The
sacred trust was never broken; she never spoke a word. Would
Lorraine die in childbirth? Was that it? Patricia dared not pray
for such a wicked thing. Lorraine did not die. Patricia then
wished that she herself might die.

When baby Cornelius was born, the girls at the hostel were
beside themselves with excitement, twittering and cooing, and
knitting bootees. Can I hold him, Mrs Cutler? Can I watch him
have his bath? Can I give him his bottle? It was a world of baby
powder and washing on the line and crying in the night. Patricia
could not bring herself to make a fuss of Cornelius. Oh, she said,
I've seen plenty of babies. I've got heaps of cousins. I hate babies,
actually, can't stand them. Cornelius cried and cried. It got to
the point where Patricia could bear it all no longer, and she crept
out of the hostel one night and walked into town where she ran
into Barry, a boy from the church, and another boy, Brian.

You're out late.

I had to do a message for Mrs Cutler.

Want to go for a ride?

So Patricia hopped into the front of the pickup between them and they drove off towards the bushfire tower. They parked near the tower, but did not get out of the pickup. They shared two cigarettes between the three of them, drank some warm beer that was under the seat. The boys burped and swore and put their arms around her. She was feeling dizzy and ill.

Somebody said you did it with the rev.

Barry said this right into Patricia's ear, and Brian threw back his head and laughed.

Not her, he said. Not this one. Don't be stupid. Do you do it? Who with? With us yeah? You wanna root, don't you? You do?

She was wet and excited and she let them tear away her pants and each one very inexpertly pushed inside her, strong, swift, hot, thrilling, meaningless and exhilarating. The pickup and the boys smelt utterly filthy like fish and mushrooms and drains and petrol and stale pee and dead things, and she liked it.

So what was your message for Mrs Cutler? You want a message for Mrs Cutler? We'll do a message for the silly old bag. Tell her we want to give her a message out at the old fire tower one of these old nights.

Patricia felt calm and pleased. She laughed with them and said OK, I'll tell her that. Will that be all?

They liked her sense of humour very much, and they laughed.

Then they drove her back to the hostel and she crept in the back kitchen door, her whole body in disarray, her feet bare, a strong smell of the night's startling activities clinging to her, moving with her.

Suddenly the lights went on and there was Father. He was standing by the kitchen table, white and stiff and wild-eyed. The hunting rifle lay diagonally across the bare white surface of the table. Was he going to kill her?

You have been with those boys. Don't lie to me. You have been with boys. This is an utter betrayal of my trust in you, of your parents' trust in you, of the love of God. You have betrayed God, Patricia, and you can no longer remain under this roof. You will go upstairs, and my wife will assist you with your packing. You will remain in the kitchen tonight, and tomorrow you will be on the first train home. Your parents and Hightower will be informed. You have disgraced your family, you have disgraced yourself. You have forfeited your scholarship – there are girls who would give their eye teeth for that scholarship. Girls who would give their right arm. You Are Nothing But a Slut. If you think you can bring your wicked filthy ways in here among pure young women you have another think coming. And his voice rose to a shriek, then fell to a whisper. Wicked, wicked, he whispered, his head quivering from side to side in little jerky spurts. Wicked, wicked. And, almost inaudible now – slut, sinful, sinful whore.

He picked up the rifle and followed her to the door, to where Lorraine was waiting at the bottom of the stairs. Lawrence pointed the rifle at Patricia's head, and then at her ankles and she began to mount the staircase, Lorraine following her. Lawrence remained at the bottom of the stairs, the rifle pointed, and Cornelius began to holler from the nursery. A lusty, haunting, terrible banshee wail.

In a trance of obedience and a kind of lucid appreciation of what had to be done, Patricia packed her case while Mother Lorraine stood beside her looking out the window into the dark sky, while the other girls stared in silent amazement from their beds. Father stood in the kitchen doorway, silent, and Patricia sat at the kitchen table. Lorraine made her wash and dress and then she made her eat some toast and drink a cup of cocoa. Patricia could barely swallow. From Lorraine she could feel a sympathy, a warmth and kindness and sorrow. But she could not cry. She felt that the lack of tears made Lawrence even more angry, if that was possible. She wished he would shoot her dead, there at the kitchen table, so it would all be over. Lorraine drove her to the station when it was time, and that was the end of Patricia's career at Hightower School .

Her parents took the word – of course they did – of Father Cutler. They curled back into their shame, afraid of the daughter who was now disgraced. In due course Patricia went to work at the local post office where every day she suffered the stares and comments of people she used to know. Patricia Calley who won a scholarship to high-brow Hightower School and slipped up on her own high opinion of herself and came home in disgrace. Pride comes before a fall. They peered at her for signs of pregnancy. Patricia could bear it no longer and finally she went to Sydney to study nursing. Her sister had long since married and gone to live in far north Queensland. Patricia kept very much to herself, until she met Kevin, had the children, and time went on.

Strange to say – or is it – she never stopped praying to God for a reunion with Lawrence Cutler. She kept a file of newspaper clippings which told the story of his glamorous career from Rural Dean to Precentor to Bishop. He and his wife Lorraine (pictured) had six children. His popularity and importance were legendary. He beamed from the pages of newspapers and glossy magazines, met the Queen, entertained Prince Charles and Princess Diana. The Princess stood beside him in a bright green silk dress with a matching hat and shoes, smiling serenely into the camera.

There came a time, however, some twenty years after she left Hightower, that Patricia found herself one morning sitting down at the kitchen table and writing a letter to Lawrence. Her life, she said, was so disastrous, Kevin so abusive, her children so distant and unloving, herself so lost – she was turning to him for any advice or assistance he could give her. He had once given her life meaning; what was his advice? She felt moved by a greater power to write this letter, still further moved to post it to the Diocesan Office. One week later she received a letter bearing a bishop's crest, and there, on the envelope, was the square black definite handwriting of Lawrence Cutler, Bishop Cutler. The shock of the sight of it made her faint, weak with a kind of fear, and dizzy with renewed desire, with gratitude to a God who listened to her, who answered her prayers at last. Please God let him write to me, let him answer my letter, let him long for me the way I long for him. Let us be together. Let it be perfect. Twenty years God listened, and when He deemed her worthy, He answered her prayers.

> *'I shall rescue you from your life of torment. The time is coming, dear one, when we shall be together. The years have passed and nothing between us has changed. Those years dissolve to nothing, like snow. Absence makes the heart grow fonder, and the time for our union is fast approaching. Please do me the loving honour of responding to my humble letter, to my fierce protestation of eternal and undying love. If I have ever hurt you, it was in the furnace of the fire of my passion for you. This is the will of God.'*

Patricia answered the letter with joy in her heart, and they exchanged many thrilling and poetic letters back and forth, back and forth. Then they arranged to meet. She left Kevin and moved into a small rented house where Lawrence came to visit her, and from where they journeyed out into the countryside in Lawrence's luxurious car, taking a picnic basket and a rug and incredible bottles of chilled French champagne and gourmet sandwiches. Strawberries in green glass dishes and blobs of luscious cream. Frolic and romp. Beneath a tree, beside a stream, dangerously public, lost in a world of their own romantic dreams, so many years since life had parted them, they were joined in love. It was like music, and it continued on for eight whole years – years of strange and secret bliss. He gave her books and flowers and jewellery and perfume. And the fox skin rug. Then Lawrence one day brought with him three large suitcases, arriving at the house in the middle of the breathless afternoon.

I have left Lorraine. She understands completely, and wants only the best for us, for you and me. I have written to the Primate, resigned from the Episcopate, given it all up. We are what matters now. God moves in a mysterious way His wonders to perform – and Lawrence said a Latin blessing. Then he giggled hysterically. Patricia wept with joy and a kind of frantic disbelief. If God had listened to Patricia's prayers, He had moved in a most un-mysterious way. The reality of all this was very clearly contained in three large leather suitcases. It was now time, Lawrence said, for them to have a child. She would carry his son and suckle him and nourish him with her body.

For several weeks they lived this story, their love-making tender and frequently concentrated on the sacred task of conception. Patricia and the Bishop and the child-to-be. But then late one morning there was a most undiscreet knock at the door, and there stood three clergymen in rigid bright black suits and shiny shiny collars. Sunglasses, yes, three big black pairs of mirrored sunglasses. There was something farcical about it all, and Patricia felt a deep and terrible choking hysteria mounting in her breast. They would not take no for an answer, these three men. There was no argument. Lawrence must return with them to the Cathedral – they had a small private plane waiting at the airstrip. Archbishop Stonycroft wished to see Lawrence as soon as possible in his office. Amazed, Patricia saw him shrink before them, and he took his suitcases, and within the hour, he was gone. It was a silent parting, like the spiriting away of one bewitched. Lawrence was collected like a disobedient child and taken home to mother.

Patricia, numb, cold, empty, sat on a chair in the back garden and allowed large tears to flow unchecked down her face as she stared, stupid, up at the sky. A few fluffy clouds drifting like feathers. Was she looking for the plane? She saw it anyway, and she could not restrain herself from attempting a feeble little wave as Lawrence and the men in black flew out of her afternoon into that feathery sky.

He would be back.

He did not come back.

She was pregnant.

She wrote to him.

He did not answer this time.

She lost the baby.

Still he did not come.

The doctor said it would have been her last child.

Betrayed by her body.

Betrayed by Lawrence .

And betrayed by God.

Kevin died.

Patricia decided to 'get on with her life'.

But life refused. She was almost destroyed, all but destroyed, destroyed by love, betrayed, again betrayed. She could not see where she went wrong. Somehow, God got it wrong. They were star-crossed lovers, star-crossed. She would sit at the kitchen table and open the old leather bag and place the letters, in their envelopes, on the table, and read them over, sometimes in order from beginning to end, sometimes at random. Her letters from him. Photographs. One by one she would kiss them. The letters lay on the grey laminex table, all of them on their thick cream paper with the bold square confident black writing my dearest heart's darling my holy sacred sweetheart juiceball sugarlips creamy cuntlips milky thighs I want to drown inside you split you open and stay up inside you forever and die inside you stuck inside you die with me my heart's bright angel.

Patricia mended the fraying fabric of the fox skin rug — using a strong curved needle she stitched the rug with thick linen thread. With nobody to talk to, nobody with whom she could discuss the story which to her was simple, to others surely incomprehensible, Patricia made up her mind to take the letters, the proof of love, the proof of the meaning of her whole life, to the only kind of authority she knew. She went to the Archbishop, the same man who had once been Bishop Stonycroft who had performed the Laying on of Hands. Patricia took the bag of letters to Archbishop Stonycroft.

It was a time when people all over the world were coming forward with stories of ancient sexual abuse by priests — people of fifty, sixty, seventy years of age were speaking out about the men who took their childhood innocence. There were questions of apology, questions of financial compensation, questions of truth and lies.

Sir, madam, we do not believe you when you say these holy men have done these wicked things, you are deluded, malicious, mad, mad, mad.

But gradually the curtains were parted, the little black demon was out of the box, the cat was out of the bag, the jig was up!

All over, Father This-That-and-The-Other.

And the gates of the prison clanged behind them and the word 'paedophile' was hissed and breathed and shouted and splashed across the papers and the TV screens. And the more you looked the more you found, and the higher up you went the worse it got. Everywhere in vestries and confessionals and deaneries and parish offices and episcopal palaces people were at work mopping up and trying to contain the flood of narrative that came spilling out from every nasty nook and cranny of every quiet sacred monastery garden and each and every sorry sandstone convent wall.

Your story does not really have the ring of truth, Mrs Shelby. I am sorry, but this is speculation and fabrication of the highest order. These letters are not evidence, I am sorry to have to tell you. They mean nothing whatsover. I am sorry you have been put to this trouble. Bluster, bluster, pop, pop, pop, bluster. The cold grey of the Archbishop's eyes was sharp as tempered steel, set in the smooth smooth shaven baby pudge of his smug bland boneless face. It occurred to him to have the woman murdered in her sleep. Steal the letters, buy the letters, and silence the woman forever. For the sake of everything that is holy, for the sake of the Anglican Communion, for the sake of Heaven, for Heaven's sake.

Patricia, who had learned, if nothing else, patience over years, sensed that her time was coming, and she persevered in hope. Dogged hope.

The woman is a dog. Nothing but a stupid, whingeing, lying, braying hound of the worst possible filthy kind. Stupid crazy bitch. Somebody get those ridiculous bloody letters the idiot wrote to her and destroy them, for Christ's sake. My God, where was his brain? Maniac. He always was a bit of a maniac, by all accounts.

But it really was too late.

Patricia was, at last, winning. The tide had turned. Stonycroft made a public statement in which he personally blamed Patricia for what had 'befallen' Lawrence Cutler. The Press Pounced. No, no, Patricia was not to blame!! – *Lawrence* was to blame. Lawrence was guilty. Lawrence had, apart from anything else, had carnal knowledge of a minor in his care. Carnal Knowledge of a Minor. Old-fashioned words came tumbling out of radios in cars, burbled out of TVs and pottered righteously around kitchens. They swam deliriously across the internet. It was a crime. The Bishop Lawrence Cutler had committed a dreadful dreadful crime. A sin too.

And silly Stonycroft had misread the temper of the times. Archbishop Stonycroft was disgraced and Bishop Cutler was not simply disgraced, but – oh strange delicious and archaic word – defrocked. All his lovely satin and embroidered chasubles twined with golden thread and decorated with vine leaves and lavish crucifixes of handsome Christs with long sorrowful hands were sent back to the dress-up box and put away forever. No more getting about in long black skirts, Lawrence. No more cassock no more surplice no more holy incense in the damp mysterious vestry. It is over now. You have been undressed in public, defrocked, defrocked. The word rang in Lawrence's brain with a horrible jagged note. Something unthinkably ridiculous had happened and he was no longer himself. With his incredibly loyal wife, he went to live in retirement, a private citizen. Why, ask many thoughtful and wondering people, why is he not in prison with all the other priestly paedophiles? And the only answer is a shrug, a raised eyebrow, a hand gesture of helpless questioning defeat.

Some memories are like hallucinations.

When Patricia takes off her coat Moira sees she is wearing a dress of muted greens and purples and browns. The mouth of the leather bag opens and the soft square cream envelopes – stamped, addressed, sealed, signed, delivered – shuffle and slither forward onto the polished surface of the dining room table.

Something Else Moira Might Say

I can't really understand why he is not in gaol, Patricia.

And Patricia Says as She Puts the Bag of Letters on the Table Beside the Old Photograph

Well, what good would that do anyway. I would just like him to say he is sorry for what he has done, what he has caused in my life, all the heartache. Here are the letters. I don't know what I am going to do with them now. I just don't know. I am keeping them, I think, because I hope that one day before he dies he will come to me and he will say he is sorry now and he is back. We will sit down together and we will read the letters, and we will be together. I will say to him – yes, Lawrence, I will take you to myself, after everything, because you have told me you are sorry, I will take you back. And he will say it is the will of God, and the love of God will succour us, and we will be at one, at peace. Set me as a seal upon thine heart, as a seal upon thine arm. For love is strong as death.

This is the truth.

MONKEY BUSINESS

Zoop-zoop. The iPhones were out in force. The video clips were uploaded to YouTube and Facebook.

People say that things drift around in cyberspace forever, so if there is still a cyberspace when all the people who were at the party are dead, even if there are no people anywhere to watch, even if there is no heaven and no earth, somewhere-somewhere, maybe, the moment will still be playable, or would be playable, somehow, supposing there were intelligent life that cared, and a working device.

It was only a small thing, in what is called the scheme of things. A small detail in that bigger picture people talk about.

A well-dressed capuchin monkey disappeared from a children's party in Melbourne. The events leading up to the disappearance, and the last view of this agile creature, were caught on camera. His alarming grin, his great dark eyes, his tail, his bottom. The story became a bit of a legend among the families of the children present, and naturally it moved far and wide out into that cyberspace mentioned before.

It was Charlotte Rose's fifth birthday party. A mighty big day in Charlotte's life, as you will see. If Charlotte (known as Charlie, but no relation to the Charlie Rose who broadcasts from the Bloomberg building in New York) lives to be ninety-five or so, providing her planet also survives, she will probably occasionally tell the story of her fifth birthday party, to her drooping dying day. It was, as it turned out, a *very* big day for Charlie.

The children at the party loved the antics of Munto the monkey. Little red fez and braided jacket. No pants. Cute! Cute! They squealed in that kissy high-pitched way little children have perfected. Munto, after dancing with his carer, Riff, executing a few melodious steps on the xylophone, and playing something like cricket with the children, came indoors to the party table. Ah, the party table. The cake had been made by Charlie's aunt, iced in green jungle leaves with the central image of a cavorting monkey in a fez. The aunt was clearly gifted with her icing bag. When they sang Happy Birthday Dear Charlie, Munto beat time with a baton. Cute! Cute! He drank a tiny glass of bright pink lemonade, then he reached down from his carer's shoulder and scooped up an exquisite little red velvet cupcake which he nibbled swiftly with his dear busy little teeth. His eyes were huge and wild. Ecstasy!

The iPhones flashed obediently and then, perhaps alarmed by the constant zoop-zoop of them, Munto went berserk. He leapt from the shoulder and, bounding as if on air up the long marble staircase, he knocked over a glass table of Art Deco Meissen figurines along the way. Leaping wild in the jungle of the mansion staircase. As it happened one of the casualties was a red stoneware monkey that bore some resemblance to Munto himself. There's coincidence for you. Insurance would cover the breakages, but the figures themselves were in fact irreplaceable. You could say they should not have been sitting there exposed to the world of little monkeys. Yes, you could say that.

Fifteen five-year-old squeals of ecstatic hysteria. 'And then,' each and every child said later to their amazed, amused and possibly horrified audiences, 'and then it stopped in front of a big statue and did a poo on the rug.' Cute! Poo!

More and higher squeaky squeals.

The monkey then flew across the landing and leapt from an open window into a tall ornamental palm. And was gone. Gone. Out the window and into the trees. Wide blue yonder. The space that had been Munto was an empty space. Oooooooh!

The party descended into chaos and even higher hysteria; the guests were hastily given cake and gift bags filled with clickers and whistles and bright red and green things to chew, and returned to their own homes. The guest of honour ran sobbing to her mother, clung to her, had to be given Phenergan and a bath and a number of toys. In PJs and robe Charlie was confined to the home theatre where she and Indigo the nanny tucked into a tray of party food and watched *Nanny McPhee and the Big Bang*. (No perceptible similarities between Indigo and Nanny McPhee. Indigo was fairly young and extremely pretty with extra-long legs and a fantastic tattoo of a rat on her right shoulder, shiny black finger and toe nails, as well she exuded a strong aroma of tobacco.)

'I did love that naughty monkey, Indigo,' Charlie said. 'He will come back, won't he? He will come back. He was so naughty. Do monkeys go to heaven, Indigo?'

Indigo said they probably did, but she also hoped, she truly hoped he would come back. Maybe, if he had been wearing pants, things might have been different, who knows? Up the marble staircase he flies, pauses for a call of nature, out the window and into the paradise of the trees, the wide blue yonder, space, time. Perhaps he was eaten by arboreal foxes. Indigo didn't know anything much about anything much. But she somehow sensed that everything, *everything*, was unravelling, going, as her grandmother would say, to hell in a handbasket. Indigo had been educated at an 'exclusive' school for girls where, at the expense of science and history and grammar, she learned principally how to survive and prevail in the treacherous millrace that is the female common-room. Heaven was as good a place as any for the monkey. Munto's handler, Riff, was Indigo's brother, and a lot of things depended on Munto. Most important of all, Indigo felt that her standing with her employers, Vanessa and Chip Rose, barristers, counted on a swift return to the status quo. Which kind of depended on the return of the monkey.

The status quo was thus: While Vanessa was conducting an on-and-off love affair with Gerald, a neighbouring professor of biology who was conveniently divorced, Chip was enjoying a delicious dalliance with (you guessed it of course) Indigo. Forget about Charlie. That was the status quo. Which was not going to return, as it happened, for poor little Munto was never seen again, and an almighty row broke out between Vanessa and Chip, using the monkey as its beginning, middle, and end. Somewhere in the middle Vanessa scooped up the fragments of the Meissen figurine and showered Chip with them as he turned on his heel and stormed out of the Tuscan limestone kitchen. (Some surfaces of the house were very unforgiving; some, such as those in the dreamlike home theatre, were soft as melting marshmallow. Oooooh!)

Munto was never ever seen again, ever, and his absence was the focus of loud and widespread chatter in the general community, which includes cyberspace. Specially cyberspace which loves such tales with their spicy pictures. A small red fez and a mound of monkey business go a long way on the web. Twitter went mad with monkey poo for a few hours. People claimed his breed was on the IUCN Red List of Endangered

Species. (In fact it wasn't, but rumour is a wonderful thing, and truth is malleable.) Riff cleared out to north Queensland where he got work on some kind of butterfly farm and gave up the idea of working with performing monkeys. Chip moved into a riverside apartment where Indigo looked after him instead of looking after Charlie (who visited every second weekend leaving Vanessa and Gerald to patter back and forth between the two large houses where they lived, separated by lawns and garden beds and trees – quite a few tall tall ornamental palms where a monkey could make his escape into the blue. Was Munto the lucky one?)

'So,' said Gerald, 'you could say the monkey became the symbol of the breakdown in the marriage.'

'Oh stop talking like a speaker at a conference, will you?' Vanessa said.

Gerald laughed. He had a great laugh, and gleaming teeth and sparkling eyes. Large hands.

'I make a point of never speaking at conferences,' he said in his soft and reasonable voice. 'Here's to monkey business. In any case, the creature was on the way out, you know. He's on the Red List.'

They proceeded to drink their tall glasses of Krug in Gerald's jacuzzi before a nice lazy afternoon in the bedroom, and dinner on the terrace. Under the stars. Was that Munto singing somewhere up in a neighbouring monkey puzzle tree? Do monkeys have any luck climbing monkey puzzles with all those deadly spikes? Probably not.

But the monkey *was*, as it happened, the symbol of the breakdown of Vanessa's marriage.

And Charlie was the casualty.

Her five-year-old status quo, such as it had been, was no more. Unlike Munto, there was no Red List on which she could possibly appear. Oh! Poor Charlie the Casualty.

When Vanessa and Gerald went to live in Southern California, Chip and Indigo moved back into the house with the Tuscan limestone kitchen and Indigo got some more fantastic tattoos. Charlie moved in with them. Charlie made an adorable flower girl in floating silver chiffon at the wedding which was at a very fashionable and romantic church (where Charlie had been christened when she was a baby in antique lace). A tall slender grey-gold spire, a lych-gate wreathed in roses. The wedding reception was at the Windsor Hotel, as was only right and proper. In the circumstances. The circumstances! Indigo decided to embellish her image by dropping her surname and taking Chip's. So she became Indigo Rose. Pretty as.

It was strange for Charlie now that Indigo had taken her mother's place in the house. But children, you know, are famous for their resilience and their ability to adapt. A new nanny came, one selected, in Indigo's wisdom, with a few of the characteristics of Nanny McPhee. Not, it has to be pointed out, the dental problems. Sharon as she was called had nice teeth and a rather pretty singing voice. She had short legs and a flat chest and she stayed for years. Sharon and Charlie would go to the park some afternoons, and Charlie liked Sharon to push her slowly, slowly like a baby on the creaky old roundabout. Slowly, slowly Charlie circled round and round – the chipped red cap in the middle of the roundabout holding the world together. Holding the world together. Yes. Slowly round and round. Push now Sharon. Slowly. The world spins. The swings and the trees are a gentle blur. The old horse and his flower cart at the corner of the park just drift along the rim of the circle of the world; the cars zipping up and down the road in the distance are ribbons of glitter, rivers of steel. Molten steel. Charlie's roundabout goes slowly round and round. And it never makes her dizzy.

As I write, Charlie is still a child, and the planet is still trundling along, the story of the party, monkey etc still cheerfully floating around out there in the lovely ether – or whatever it is – of cyberspace. Munto had his few minutes of fame, and continues to have them. I think he retains his status as the symbol of the breakdown of the marriage, as Gerald put it. The lives of Chip and Indigo, Gerald and Vanessa, Riff and Charlie are fairly routine in their way. Riff's butterfly business in north Queensland seems to be booming. Then there was Sharon – her life too, you realise, was changed by the disappearance of Munto the Monkey. The only really interesting thing I can tell you about them all is that Indigo Rose became a force to be reckoned with in the Melbourne real estate business, and rightly famous also for her fabulous tattoos of which there came to be many more than that original rat.

Charlie is intensely interested in animals – collects dogs, cats, guinea pigs, horses, chickens, lizards, unicorns – and I predict that she will become a vet, maybe, or an animal rights' activist. Time will tell, as it usually does. For now, things are fairly settled. Status quo. Zoop-zoop.

Imaginary Coda

And so in the end Charlie Rose lived happily ever after. Life had its ups and downs. She lived another ninety years after the party, and she often told the story of Munto the monkey. It seemed to be the turning point, the focus, the high, the low. In the end, everything that was Charlie Rose turned slowly round and round that central point. Among her treasures was a small framed photographic print of Munto with the red velvet cupcake in his paw. Dear little Munto with the dark burgundy crumbs of the sponge on his lips. Poor little Munto. Look, look at his sweet little teeth, his crimson fez, his tail, his glee. His terror. The terror in his eyes. Cute! The terror in his eyes.

PERHAPS THAT BIRD WAS WISE

She is a child again, Allegra, now skipping along the path to the front of the house, like the girl on the cover of the book of fairy tales, now pressing her ear to the tick tick tick of her mother's wrist watch, such a pretty thing, the watch, small and glittering marcasite, just fool's gold her mother says, fool's gold, Allegra, but pretty and winking, and it tells the time, and they used to make marcasite jewellery long ago in ancient Greece.

In the early hours of the late spring morning, Gwen died, as everyone said, peacefully in her sleep. Her daughter Allegra supposed they could tell because the bedclothes were probably undisturbed. It was Harry, Allegra's husband, who found Gwen still and cold in her wide oak bed, the radio lying face-up on the coverlet, softly playing a Bach sonata. Her marcasite watch still ticking and glittering on her twiggy wrist, almost audible in the silence. Tiny glinting watch, hanging loosely on the tiny shrunken wrist. Harry later said he was sort of transfixed by the watch, so that he stood beside the bed for what seemed like an eternity before turning and fleeing down the stairs to make his announcement of Gwen's passing. Peacefully in her sleep. 'Passing' did seem to be the appropriate word. She had somehow slid away from them, from everything, from the single glass of water on her night-table, from the silver statue of the Little Mermaid next to it. Heart failure. Is that peaceful? Perhaps it is. Slid away. Slid away.

Allegra is a child again, sliding down astride the banister, skipping up the stairs again, slipping sideways into mother's bedroom, smoothing her hand over the Little Mermaid, kissing the crystal box where the twinky winky watch goes to sleep at night.

It was raining on the day of the funeral. Allegra thought this was apt, like a funeral in a movie, raining, with umbrellas. When people were winding their solemn ways towards the house, through the garden afterwards, Allegra was waiting on the verandah to greet them. They came forward slowly, lugubriously, visible only, from where she was standing, as the shining mushroom shapes of wet umbrellas, most of them silky black, one bobbing lipstick pink, one imprinted with a joyful painting by Renoir. The contrast of the pink and the painting with the black made the black more emphatically mournful. Yes, lugubrious. The garden was dense and overgrown, roses heavy with raindrops, foliage drooping in great swoops, bending low over the brick path. In fact people had to push their way through from the gate, down the slope, to the house. They shook the umbrellas, showering the verandah with sprinklings and sprays of water. Some stretched them out to dry, others folded them and stood them, handle up, to drip into the iron dragon umbrella-stand by the door.

Allegra is a child again, quietly licking the film of dust from the spines on the dragon's old green skin. She can hear the murmur, babble and shriek of the funeral people as they puddle and pierce the air with their memories and opinions, Gwen was a dear, dear friend, mother, wife, sister, worker of good in the community, think of the Red Cross and she was always there, always ready with a smile and a kind word, always punctual, such a good knitter.

In the weeks when Gwen was dying in the Melbourne house, Allegra stayed with her in the solid Victorian place where Allegra and her brothers grew up. She and Harry slept in the big guest bedroom, next door to the room where she had slept as a child. In the short-hand language of real estate, the house had the return verandah, the iron lace, the vast high ceilings, the marble fireplaces, the hand-painted birds and flowers on the glass around the door, the sixteen-inch skirting boards, the ceiling roses. The brothers were there, one having flown in from Brussels, one from far north Queensland. They worked with Harry on the smooth running of the whole thing, the big picture as it were, while Allegra did the details of announcements in papers, the order of the service, the choice of hymns, the flowers for the church, food and drink (oh such sandwiches, such petits fours) tablecloths and napkins, china and glasses, silver, what to wear, what to say. Ritual and routine came to her rescue. There were many children of all ages. Allegra and Harry's two girls, some cousins, almost everyone. They had loved Gwen who was strict but kind. A medicine cabinet replete with Betadine and Savlon and Bandaids and everything under the sun for sunburn and insect bites and asthma and headache and constipation. Allegra cried a lot. She could of course be forgiven for that. Her mother had died.

She decided to wind the marcasite watch, not let it stop, never let it stop keep it going. She did this secretly, kept the watch in its crystal box in a drawer of the rosewood chest in the guest room. It was not a valuable watch, but rich in sentiment. Gwen's parents had given it to her for her sixteenth birthday. It did occur to Allegra, frequently, that if she kept the watch going for the rest of her life, then it would eventually, in the course of time, the natural sequence of events, stop some time after her own death. Her own death. Like that old song about the grandfather's clock. Stopped short, never-to-go-again, when the old man died. Time, Allegra realised, perhaps for the first time at the age of fifty, was not elastic, and was not long. Time was short. It had the winged chariot. After a few days she decided to wear the watch, discarding the round gold one she had worn for many years. The marcasite felt insubstantial, strange, old-fashioned, princessy. But the time was real. It fitted her as it had not fitted skinny shrinking Gwen in those final horrible weeks.

There were many sayings, some from childhood, Gwen's sayings, that came drifting and insisting into Allegra's mind as she went about the business of sifting and sorting and packing and disposing – dispersing the fabric of the world of things that Gwen had gathered about her.

Allegra is a child again. She hears her mother say: 'Everything comes to those who wait.' Allegra now knows exactly what that means. It doesn't really mean that if you are patient at the dinner table you too will receive your portion of apple pie with cloves and ice-cream. Doesn't really mean that if you stop whining about needing a blue velvet dress you will get one quicker. No, it means that in the end you will get the little watch that you have loved so much, and that then you will die and cease to be and the watch can go on and on, and somebody – maybe some other patient person – can wear it in their turn, since they are waiting. And later on they will die. All the ancient Greeks are dead now.

'Everything happens to everybody.' That was Gwen's other principal saying, and Allegra had always known it was bleak and sinister. Death comes in the end – but did the end come at the end? Had the story-so-far really been properly developed, properly told? What were the Fates up to with their threads and their snip-scissors? Did they know what they were doing? Was it *time*? Were they playing at time?

Allegra the sensible adult holds in her hand the ticking watch in its crystal box. She speaks to it: 'I have always wanted to play the cello; I have always wanted to go to China; I have always wanted to climb the leaning tower of Pisa, read *War and Peace*, go walking in Tasmania, go to Uluru. The party can't really be over, can it, until I have fitted these things in?'

Allegra had some other vague desires, a kind of longing to live for years in simple luxury in Italy, for instance, but this was, she realised, what is known as a 'pipe dream', Italy a place she could really reach only when in some kind of opium-induced trance. But there was one wish that she had had since childhood, buried for many years in the overlay of life's hurtling necessities. It came back to her in the last weeks of her mother's illness.

As Gwen lay, sometimes quiet, sometimes querulous, sometimes fretful in the upstairs bedroom, the big window open onto the Juliet balcony, Allegra had taken to reading to her from the old book of fairy tales. There is the girl on the cover, skipping along the winding path up to the front door, flowers blooming in bright profusion beside the pathway. Gwen was soothed by the sound of Allegra's voice, she smiled and drifted, sometimes asking a question, making a sharp comment. 'Really, how could she walk, let alone dance, in a slipper made of glass? What do you think it really means – *happily ever after*? I have always wondered.' She was not very demanding, and there was something unsettling about this fact. You could placate her with a small vase of marigolds or a freshly laundered lace handkerchief. The illustrations in the book were by Frederick

Richardson, and when Allegra came to the pictures of the Three Bears she found that tears sprang to her eyes. For there was the image she had carried in her heart since childhood – the bears in their ideal house. Oh the awful disruption of Goldilocks.

Allegra is a child again. That is where I always want to live, that's where I will live, in the drawing of the inside of the house of the Three Bears. I love the chairs. It's the chairs that I want. I want to hop up on one of the chairs and settle my bottom, and face the table and be on that chair. Who's been sitting in my chair?

Those solid, red-brown, child's idea of a chair with arm-rests. Of course the bears' chairs were in three different sizes, but that was not the point. As she gazed at the illustrations, the adult Allegra longed for chairs, six maybe, matching in size, large, blocky, and red-brown. The statement of chair. The essence of chair. Allegra would sit at one end of the table, and Harry at the other, and the girls and their partners along the sides. One day the girls and their children. As she looked at the pictures she would take the whole scene to somewhere in Italy, Tuscany perhaps, or the Amalfi coast, and there they would be in the kitchen of the Three Bears' House, sitting on the red-brown chairs, eating something better than porridge from big white bowls with blue bands around the edge. 'Why have you stopped reading?' Gwen said. 'Go on. I like "The Straw Ox". Show me the pictures.'

In the days after the funeral Allegra picked up the book and turned to 'The Three Bears'. She sat on the bed and turned the pages. Goldilocks peering in at the door, the chairs in all their red-brown seriousness waiting for her. An interesting thing about pipe dreams is that they often work best if they remain in their own poppied element, stay glimmering in their insubstantial dream-medium, never see the light of day, so harsh, sometimes, and unforgiving. For there is actually no real reason why Allegra could not have taken the picture, say, to a carpenter and ordered a set of kitchen chairs. But the dreamer loves the dream. And isn't there a poem by Eliot where a bird says that humans can't take too much reality? Where does Allegra stand on reality these days as she slips and slides in and out of her pipe dreams?

Perhaps that bird was wise.

It was about two years after Gwen died, two years after the days with the Three Bears and their lovely old red chairs, when the watch was still ticking, and life goes on, when each of the girls had produced golden-haired sons, that chance, fate – or perhaps the power of dream – took Allegra and Harry on a drive in the country one Sunday afternoon.

You (and I) know that Allegra is going to be confronted with the chairs, now that she is taking a little journey into the land of antique shops, don't you, don't I? But Allegra did not know.

They had passed several cute antique shops in sleepy towns when Harry said he needed coffee and was going to stop at the next ye olde café. They pulled up at Collette's Café and had long blacks and incredibly good ginger biscuits. Then they went next door to The Fox's Lair, where, in a back room, they found four red-brown kitchen chairs with arm-rests. Yes. Imagine. The chairs. Right there just waiting in The Fox's Lair. A dream come true. Only four? Harry said. What's the good of four? With the girls and their families and everyone. But four it was, and they arranged for a carrier to deliver them. Such practicalities. Such a delicious tasting of fairy tale, myth, bouncing forward into the reality of the light of common day.

Allegra went into a state of breathless disbelief. Her chairs were coming. And they did. Before you could say Frederick Richardson, in the twinkling of an eye, there they were, lined up around the kitchen table. The man said he had had them for years, didn't recall where they had come from. Harry said he thought they looked a bit odd and maybe silly mixed up with the four old bentwoods. A neighbour admired them and said she had a man in Eltham who could make some more. So more were made. Eight red chairs around the kitchen table. Allegra still could scarcely believe it all. People said they were beautiful and amazing, and what an eye Allegra had for just the right thing at the right time. Allegra never, not even to Harry, explained that the chairs were a manifestation of some magical workings quite beyond her ken. They had been in the dream-making for nearly fifty years, elves tap-tapping away at them, dipping their brushes into their paint pots of lovely dark red paint.

Christmas dinner, always held at the kitchen table, that year was, to Allegra, a kind of secret celebration of the chairs. Her heart was warm and smug, and somehow happily ever after had gently come to pass. She settled her bottom onto the seat of her red chair. She had made her mother's Christmas pudding, marked in the old hand-written recipe book as 'My pudding, very good', alongside other puddings labelled 'Davina's easy pudding', 'Mrs Trethewey's pudding', neither of which was given any kind of rating. Allegra was at one end of the table, Harry at the other, Lizzie and George and baby Jake, Charlotte and Rob and baby Edward along the sides. Eight. A magic number. The golden carousel of angels flying above burning candles in the centre of the table, round and round they whirl.

Everything comes to those who wait.

Allegra is a child again. She is wearing the tick tick tick of her mother's dear old watch. Fool's gold, Allegra, fool's gold, so pretty, so twinkly, since the time of the ancient Greeks.

And everything happens to everybody.

WHERE THE HONEY MEETS THE AIR

I call her Honey-Hannah and she calls me Sugar-Sam. It's pretty sweet at our place.

And you know how it is with honey.

I hope you do.

Otherwise we're not going to be on the same page for a while here.

Follow…ME.

You see it there in the bowl, pot, with the honeybee embossed – is that the word – on the side that curves and fits in the palm of your hand – and you take the silver spoon they gave you when you were born – that was a while ago now wasn't it – maybe your were actually born with it in your mouth (joke) – and you dig into the viscous – I think that's what it is, viscous, sounds good – viscous semi-liquid – it doesn't resist – down goes the soft sharp side of the silver spoon (Shakespeare? – joke) and you hold it just above your toast all buttery and gleaming in the light of the conservatory, and you let that honey run drip dribble flow manifest down onto the butter, the toast – and it glides and pools and glows, positively literally *glows* as if lit from within – and you think of a word and in the beginning it was, and the word was 'meniscus' and you wonder, there at the late morning breakfast table, if honey can be said to do meniscus, so you whip out the iPad (to tell the truth it was already there, whipped, all along) and off you go to Wikipedia and you're a little bit the wiser because now you kind of know that the 'meniscus', plural menisci, from the Greek 'crescent', is the curve in the upper surface of a liquid close to the surface of the container, caused by the surface tension, and depending on the liquid and the surface' – oh blah blah there's lots more but that's enough of that kind of talk really, for now – and I conclude that meniscus wasn't what I was looking for was it – I'm just thinking of the *skin* of the honey aren't I – the part where the honey meets the air and where it kind of resists something – pressure? moisture? distant laughter? – in the air, so that faint striations (OMG the old vocabulary is choofing along this morning) of heavenly pale butter beginning ever so delicately to marble (too heavy, this marble word) the envelope of the honey, and it is nearly time (tick tock/ ayers rock/silver slippers/ brighton rock – Shakespeare again) to put the spoon somewhere – where – not back in the honey, surely – oh bugger it, put it back in the honey and hang it all if some butter or a crumb of toast or the vestige of the dry wing of a dead moth happens to land in there – or an ant, what about an ant? have signals gone out to the bloody ants letting them know that the honey pot – pot or bowl? jar? – oh English it's so devilish isn't it – now if this were French the honey would be, I imagine, simply in a compotier de miel or some such and be done with it, unless some froggy whiz had siphoned it onto a soucoupe (yes I tried to look it up but if I faff around in the French/English, English/French for much longer we'll be here all day and never get to put the toast and honey into anybody's mouth, let alone mine) – but the funny thing was that not far from 'miel' there lay a squashed and desiccated *ant* caught in the pages of the big

Larousse, and highlighting the word 'mignarder' which apparently is Frog for to pat, to caress, to fondle – I liked the sound of that – and it goes on to explain that if you do this thing called 'mignarder son style' (yes I too thought we had wandered into porno there, patting the stylus, but no) you are being *finical* – I could leave you to look up finical in your Shorter Oxford (get real, mister – look it up on google) but to save time I will tell you it means to be affectedly fastidious or precise in one's use of language, and to engage in mincing metaphors (OMG!! – 'mincing metaphors'!!!! exclamation mark – think of the dead ant – a metaphor, but is it mincing?) and I feel a figure of speech coming on in any case because the wing of the moth (imaginary) set me thinking that the honey is quite similar to amber, isn't it, and what do you know – we called our baby daughter Amber, yes indeed we did – to Hannah and Sam, a baby girl – her eyes are as brown (simile alert) as – as what – oh you fill in the blanks – and her lips are as red as – oh no! – blood – some old fairy tale, I imagine it's Snow White, is crossing wires with me and a witch or wicked queen or step-mother is planning to hook our baby (she's now nearly two years old BTW and is partial to a spot of toast and honey herself, pat, pat, caress, caress) up with a prince from some minor kingdom by the sea in the distant or not so distant future of the planet, supposing the poor old planet has a future which maybe it does and maybe it doesn't, all things considered, what with the morphing climate and the disappearing bees (bee motif) and the way the sea is rising up like King Neptune reclaiming his rights whatever they were, and the way the sun is a dying star (have I got that right – oh sometimes I don't seem to know what I am talking about) – and anyhow we were living together for a yonk, me and Honey-Hannah, and happy as two little bees in lavender (that didn't really work, did it – never mind) when one day HH who had not sighted blood as red as blood for a while came out of the ensuite with a funny look on her face and a funny thing in her hand and said she thought she might be pregnant and she was of course and so we thought we'd zip off to the registry office and tie the knot – something that went out of fashion for a few years, but has come back with a vengeance in the form of the Wedding Industry of which more a bit later – when Her Family swept in and tied us up in knots, ribbons, bows and a certain amount of barbed wire, and whirled us up the aisle of St Francis in the Jolly Old Fields with a *huge* reception at Quoile, the (her) family home in the rolling hills (have I got that right, Family?) behind Kyneton in Central Victoria, Quoile being named after an old old castle in County Down where the Family had its Elizabethan roots (joke) – we are the Gunns of Quoile Castle – yes she is Hannah-Margot Gunn of Gunn's Constructions (not to mention Gunns Wedding Bells, Gunns Hardware and Gunns Honey, and not to forget Wishart, and Gunn, Barristers and Solicitors) – I should have warned you about how this narrative will tie itself up in the knots of several metaphors and coincidences and things – but Honey-Hannah is unlike most members of the Family – unlike particularly in the matter of issue – her mad sister has no children (not a hope in hell) – her brother's mad wife will have no children (although the brother, Fabian, has probably fathered a bastard or two but they would not count as your proper Gunns or Quoiles) and so when HH put forward the idea of the coming of Baby Amber there was much joyful to-do among the constructors and wedding-meisters and hard-ware handlers and apiarists (at last a real word) and barristers and solicitors, and we were propelled together into the floral archways of matrimony until death did us part (relax, we are still buzzing along nicely in the real world) unlike – oh-oh, here it comes, the fly in the ointment, the snake in the grass, the ant in the honey, the startled grasshopper in the amber – who's divorced, who's *dead* around here? who got together and then got parted by something other than death? – well, in fact it was death – this is why I'm actually at home in the conservatory thinking about honey on toast instead of going to the office I occupy in Gunns Constructions where I hold a very responsible position and where I spend a hell of a lot of my time writing plays – wha-at? – yes, that's what I do as I sit at my vast mahogany desk-a-rama, I tap away at my plays, some of which (hem-hem) have had readings at places such as the Court House and fortyfivedownstairs, while Sheba my personal secretary takes calls and takes care of all stuff such as email and – well – business – Sheba's the real thing, I just draw the salary and look good – I should explain that I am generally considered to be very presentable, a fucking asset to the whole shebang (ha ha – look at that will you – Sheba runs the whole Shebang – I just thought of that – I had occasion to text her just now to tell her I'll be late and she texts back saying – you'll like this I think – saying Take Your Time Solomon, Sheba Runs the Show) you will have seen pics of HH and me around the place – at the opera, at the races, at the charity fashion thingie, at the opening of the super awful reception for minor lovely royalty etc etc – we get around – and the great thing is we get around *together* as a genuine social item, an item in every way – HH and SS and their adorable Baby Amber – unlike, as I have intimated just now, unlike Patrick my best friend from school so long ago, unlike Patrick who has – not to put too fine a point on it – who has – um – quite recently murdered his wife Cressida – wh-at? oh yes, he did it alright – and if you don't know the story I should briefly fill you in – I warn you – it's ugly – and it's probably just as well you've got me with my finical phrasing – I will caress you as we go – pat pat, mincing metaphor notwithstanding – I will tell you the tale of Patrick and Cressida, one of whom lies at the bottom of the pool with her dead lover, and one of whom lies very much alive, telling himself long lies, just along the hallway, in my bedroom, watching who knows what on TV and drinking scotch and waiting for me to bring him toast and honey and good news as he waits for Deke Perpendicular to arrive with advice and the good oil and the loophole in the noose (I think my mincing metaphor has sidled off somewhere – and anyway we don't do the noose or any other form of capital punishment in our light and enlightened social system) – look his name isn't really Perpendicular but it's something weirdly Greek and I can't think it or spell it and so I am writing Perpendicular, emphasis on the 'dic' because in fact he is one in many ways, but in the matter of getting people out of situations as sticky as that in which Patrick finds himself, he's almost magic – so, for want of anything better to do, and as a displacement activity, and because this is how I think in a crisis – OMG but is this a crisis!! – I'm watching honey running slowly off the spoon while Patrick is in my bedroom, as I said, and I don't know what he's thinking, but I'm actually trying to distract myself from thinking about how Cressida was having this hot affair with Damien Bliss (I know, I know, but that was the name) who was the hot topic that looked after their indoor pool (heated) and everybody knew except Patrick and guess what there comes a time when Patrick arrives home in the middle of the day because he suffers from asthma (mild) and he was suffering from it, and – look I apologise for the banality of all this – but this is why Patrick is lying in the comfort of my bedroom waiting for his toast and honey and short black – so he was feeling pretty seedy and he goes in the front door and what does he see but the naked Cressida and the naked Damien hotly engaged in a soixante-neuf on the dark and wonderful Turkish rug *just inside the front door* – that was apparently, according to Patrick, what got to him – and the shock did wonders for the asthma – it was the location you see that got to him, and so to cut a long story short he loses it and he grabs Cress by her long chestnut locks with such sudden force that he breaks her neck, and then he king-hits dazed Damien who cracks his stupid head on something or other (Patrick isn't yet clear on this) and he doesn't get up either – and so what does Patrick do then – you'd wonder, wouldn't you – well he drags them one by one across the floor leaving trails of blood and stuff – and chucks them in the pool – incredible, mad, but you never know how these things will take you – I said they were on the bottom but I don't really know do I – maybe they're floating around like blow-up toys – I don't know how long the various processes take, what with the body and the water and the air and Archimedes' Principle and so on – what Patrick did was pretty amazing when you think about it – just goes to show what rage can do – then he rings me – of course he does – and I ring Perpendicular, and Patrick makes what is probably a mistake – even I can see that – he gets back in his car and comes around here where I'm getting ready to go to the office for a late morning meeting, and where I put him to bed and give him the scotch and start making toast – and so far nobody has called the police, but anyhow Perpendicular can work all that out and what I'm really waiting for is for Patrick to have his toast and get the hell out of here and then I'm going to message Sheba again and tell her I'm *really* going to be late-late, like not coming in until tomorrow week, and I'm going to go and get HH from her mad sister's where she's making quince and elderberry something or other (a quaint lot, the Quoile Gunns) and I'm going to collect Amber from Brighton Bambini and we'll drive out to Quoile and stay for a few days because in spite of anything I might have said, if there is one place I can feel safe and sound and silver-plated it's behind the great iron gates and up the winding tree-lined drive of the Family Home where Hannah's mama and also old nanny will enfold us in an incredibly stilling and sticky form of love – yes love – and nothing can ever disturb the knot of us – where no Mr Bliss can ever come, where – wait for it – here comes a rushing wave of somewhat mincing metaphors – we will be enfolded in the sweetieness of our own slow flowing honey, and we will live happily, ever after, in love and eternal ease – OMG what dismal dismal bullshit all this is – because I know, and Patrick knows, and Perpendicular knows, and the police are *going* to know, and even you know – what has happened to Patrick (has it happened to Patrick, is that it? or has Patrick *done* it – this remains to be sorted out by lawyer and police and jury and judge etc, not to mention the merry media, social and anti-social) could conceivably happen to anybody, and when you say anybody you could mean me – it could happen to me – I could come home one day and find HH in the arms (so to speak – I can't go further than that) of, say, Deke Perpendicular (laughter), and I could lose it and I could, say, shoot them with some handy gun or other and there I would be, rushing off to somebody's conservatory for scotch and toast and honey – oh yes, honey – and I could dip the spoon into the honey and I could lift up the spoon (silver, remember) and I could watch as the honey slowly falls and makes its way down onto the golden and buttery toast and I could think about bees and ants and I could wonder about the surface of the honey and I could ask a kind of question about what happens in the universe (picking up some crossed wires from Hannah's mad bad sister of the quince and elderberry concoction who has a habit of saying – oooh – everybody *dies* in the end) what happens in the universe when the honey meets the air, or you could say when the shit hits the fan – I prefer to meditate on the honey – what happens when the honey meets the air.

Yes, I could wonder about that.

SUDDEN DEATH

Maggie had sometimes wondered about Dom's love life – as if they had ever been an item – he was always the boy nextdoor – the paling fence between the old Californian bungalows in Ashburton was full of gaps big enough for them to move easily back and forth. Children always on a mission to derive the most fun out of life from dawn to dusk and afterwards. Both the youngest in families where the older ones had grown up and disappeared into the adult world. They had a string rigged up between their bedrooms and sent messages and lollies down the wire. They were a scary pair of ghosts at Halloween. One Christmas they had climbed the peppercorn in Maggie's garden and strung coloured lights connected to Maggie's father's shed across to the gum tree in Dom's garden. In high summer the front gardens were a riot with purple jacaranda, scarlet flame tree, golden silky oak and the smell of dust and hot hot sun on dry dry gum leaves. Quite often they smoked behind the cypress hedge. In the evenings the smoke and smell of barbecues – the sun goes down and the barbecue aprons come out – shouts and laughter and slabs of beer. They rode their bikes together around the streets and down to the swimming pool – were often in the same class at school. Dom was good at Maths and Maggie was good at English – they did their homework together, working out just how much they could swap and get away with it. They always got away with it. There was a particular part of the roof at the side of Dom's place where they would climb up and take turns in jumping off. It was called 'catch me' and sometimes 'catch me if I fall'. Maggie's mother was nervous and said she shouldn't play it, but Maggie and Dom took no notice. They ruined a prized clematis, smashing it as they fell backwards together – and Maggie broke her arm and they were in serious trouble. The words 'catch me if I fall' Dom wrote on her home-work diary in red and green pen, and these were the words they often said when they parted to go their different ways – little ways at first – then big ways in life. It got to be the year 2001.

Seven years before, on her twenty-first – a rowdy affair in the back garden – Dom gave Maggie a silver necklace with a pendant – a jointed fish, articulated, and a slender key that dangled and clinked against the fish. She was wearing the pendant now, slipping the fish between her thumb and fore-finger, bending it slightly this way and that, as she sat at the bar of La Vache Qui Rit on John Street New York, waiting for Dom. Late breakfast at La Vache Qui Rit.

On this bright sunny morning, clean and even sparkling, Maggie was wearing a crisp white shirt and her Jack and Jones jeans – feeling good. Back in the hotel room was the new green dress she planned to wear later on to dinner. Dinner with Dom – nice. The dress was almost the same shade as the one she had and loved when she was ten – a fresh minty silk, dreamy, soft, low cut and clinging – extra special – Collette Dinnegan – two lls two tts two nns – with incredible silver sandals. To match the fish? Maggie's freckles had faded as she grew up – her hair had deepened from pale carrot to a kind of caramel. Dom had never called her Carrots, but plenty of people had. And here she was now in the Big Apple for an interview at *Vogue*. Imagine, me, Maggie, writing for *Vogue* New York. Why not imagine me? Sent Dom an email 'catch me if I fall'. His reply 'meet you at vache for breakfast'. He was, his mother said, currently seeing a woman in banking – Dom worked in the world of finance – lived in a brownstone in Jackson Heights. It's a bit obvious and mad to say all this was a long way from the jacaranda-silky oak-flametrees of Ashburton, but, well, it was, wasn't it. A long way. That word brownstone made little shivers shiver behind Maggie's eyes. A brownstone in Jackson Heights his mother had said. And his mother didn't even really know exactly what that meant.

Maggie was on her second cup of coffee at the bar waiting for a table – the clatter and buzz of La Vache Qui Rit – wait here to be seated the waiter told her – Dom would soon be on his way – the image of the green dress in the hotel closet – once they had done that thing kids do with razor blades and wrists – tiny beads of blood mingled – murmurs beside the fish pond of forever and ever after and race you to the gate. His mother said the woman banker was called Shelagh – came from Arizona – Maggie felt old jealousy snipping through her blood – how silly – then the image of the green dress would appear in her imagination like a moth fluttering softly on the clothes line – and she was back in Ashburton and it was Dom's sixteenth and the parents were out somewhere and all the boys were drinking beer and the girls were into crystal glasses of Midori Illusions – there were UDL cans and cans of Bourbon and Coke – many glasses were smashed, and more than one person threw up in the fish pond and yes the fish probably died as a result. It was a party that became famous all around the neighbourhood – the night the Golding boy and his friends set fire to the paling fence. Dom got with revolting Shona Jones, and Maggie was deep in misery but not supposed to show it – she was nothing to Dom he was nothing to her – except they were deep down everything and never to be separated. Blood forever. Childish pledge. It was crazy how Shelagh from Banking and Shona from Glen Iris flipped in and out of Maggie's mind's eye and darted up and down her heartstrings as the waiter refilled her cup for the third time with beautiful coffee – Dom was standing in the doorway of Shelagh's office. Dom was smiling his crooked smile – he was holding out his arm and they crossed wrists, Dom and Shelagh, and big beads of bright blood mingled and a drop fell on white carpet – did they have white carpet in offices in Banking – well where was Shona Jones now – not planning to go to the office of *Vogue* in a dark suit and Manolo Blahniks at two pm and doubtless-probably-possibly-maybe-perhaps get a job on the staff – but what did it matter where Shona was when Shelagh was in her office looking out over Manhattan mingling her horrible rich-successful blood with the sweet blood of Dominic Golding in Finance. Blood that also ran blp-blp blp-blp in Maggie's veins. Except for all it mattered, Shona and Shelagh were one and the same – get over it, Maggie Willis, get over yourself – go and be seated like an adult and order – what – a panier pour un or a panier pour deux? Deux? Deux? Chausson aux pommes? Tears were starting to well up in her eyes. Damn. Prickle prickle stupid tears. She was lonely, she was alone in New York, she was Maggie from Ashburton and she was being stood up by bloody Dom Golden from number twelve and who did he think he was – she would have to SMS him soon – she couldn't stand this – falling apart at the bar in La Vache Qui Rit waiting to be seated. Be seated and get a panier pour deux and eat the lot and throw up in the fish pond at *Vogue*. One of the fish ponds at *Vogue*.

Come to think of it what was really holding him up – jealous fantasy aside? If he didn't come soon the waiter was no doubt going to give up on his 'wait here to be seated' and Maggie was going to slink sadly off into the thrum and hype of John Street. Send him an SMS? So what was she? Tryhard? Loser? Was she going to interrupt him in the middle of a sudden early morning emergency meeting or a sudden bloodbrother ceremony or worse (worse) with Shelaghinbanking. The mintygreensilkdress was beginning to droop on its clothes line – the gentle breeze had dropped and the mothlike folds of the winglike sleeves began to resemble an old school dress scrunched in a ball and stuffed into a backpack with old banana skins and leaking felt pens. To tell the truth Maggie had always had a problem with waiting – in spite of her carefree childhood among the flame trees and the barbecues and the Midori Illusions, anxiety was actually her thing – Dom was chronically unpunctual – she knew that, didn't she – yes but yes but. He was late. Bloody hell, he was late.

So Maggie sat there fingering the lovely little silver fish and the dear little silver key on the thin silver chain around her neck. She was starting to stress out on all the caffeine – she half composed the message in her head, half serious, half jokey 'got here early – waiting to be seated – catch me if I fall' – and took out her phone.

This was at precisely eight forty-six – it said so on her phone – and that was when the first plane hit the first tower. In the riot, confusion and hysteria that broke out all around her Maggie never sent the message. And at eight fifty-six her phone rang. It was Dom, an SMS.

'It's ok am in the other tower'

It was the last message Dom Golding ever sent – and the ash that went through Maggie's hotel destroyed the minty green dress too.

HARE

The Facts

Ginny Peach was shot dead in her studio. It happened in the early hours of the morning following the opening of her show 'Morning Hare'. A single bullet to the head. Six of the paintings, all pictures of hares, some black, some white, some red, some accompanied by the blurred figure of a titian-haired woman, had also been shot. The hares all had holes between the eyes. Somebody was a very good shot. The paintings resembled in style, a little, the work of Arthur Boyd. Everybody said that. The price went up after the shooting, but that was no use to Ginny. She must have known her killer, the police said, since there was no evidence of forced entry. Such is the useful language of a police investigation – killer, forced entry. The weapon was a hunting rifle. All this took place in the bush on the outskirts of the Victorian city of Bendigo, in Santa Monica Gully. It didn't take long for the police to make their way to the home of Dan Tasco, a twenty-minute drive from Ginny's studio down a rough bush track. He was taken in for questioning – more useful language – and before long was charged with murder. They never found the rifle. What can have possessed him, people wondered. He had been his usual self at the opening, Ginny's good friend and neighbour. You just never know, do you. Of course he had never really been the same since his wife died – well, disappeared. Mad with grief some people said. Others whispered that he had – as it were – done away with her. A wide area had been searched, police descending into the earth where dangerous old gold mines offered possibilities and secrets. It was a good five years since all that happened, and there was no fresh evidence, although the case was naturally still very much open. A week or so after Dan was charged he wrote a rambling confession that would answer people's questions, up to a point, but would pose deeper mysteries of its own. There would be many mysteries, seemingly related. Intertwined. Were they related? Unanswered questions. Dan said he couldn't recall what he had done with the gun. He didn't remember going to the studio or going home. But he knew he shot Ginny Peach. He said she had it coming, obviously, he said. Why? She just did. It was obvious. It was clear that Dan was not his usual easy-going self. They searched the dam at the bottom of the hill on Dan's property. Again. Five years earlier divers had done all that. Looking for a body. To no avail. His lawyer – it was Elizabeth McGee from the old firm of McGee and Moffet in Bendigo – had advised him most strongly against writing the confession, but Dan insisted he had to get everything off his chest. Elizabeth was an old girlfriend. She knew him very well. She said what he wrote was too wild and out of control, even though it did contain the confession about the shooting. Poor Dan, she thought, marrying that loopy Arielle. Elizabeth actually believed he hadn't done the shooting. Ginny had plenty of enemies about the place, and it could have been any of them. Persons unknown. No, Elizabeth said, Dan didn't do it. No, he's not himself, not his usual self, but this thing doesn't add up. He couldn't have done it, it just wasn't in him to do a thing like that, and where is the gun? First find the rifle. And how did he get from his farm to the studio and back in the time frame when his ute was on blocks? A mate had driven him to the opening and back. It made no sense. That's what Elizabeth said.

Dan Tasco's Confession

My late wife Arielle – well, I say 'late wife', but in fact there is no real guarantee she's dead. Missing. Arielle is missing. I understand that Ginny's dead. Yes, she's dead alright. That's quite straightforward. They found Arielle's iPod in the scrub near the old Starlight mine – defunct of course, the mine. The only thing on the iPod was somebody reading *Wuthering Heights*. I could have told them that. She was crazy about that book. She's been missing for nearly five years now. I think of her as dead, you know. I dream about her lovely long red hair. Titian. It's one of those stories – a woman sets out in the early morning light to go for a walk in the bush. She did this walk just about every day, ever since we moved here to the central goldfields and started growing the sunflowers. Rivers and fields of pure gold, Arielle said. She was poetic. She sets out in the early morning light. Never comes home. You hear about people who go missing and clear off to Sydney and start a whole new life with a new family and a job in IT or something. Or else they end up in a shallow grave just off the highway somewhere, and their bodies are traced by the smart phones in their jeans. Easy. But Arielle never had a smart phone. She didn't even have an email address. She sometimes used the laptop to send emails via my address, but not very often. She was, as maybe her name suggests, a bit airy-fairy, not down to earth, dreamy. Well, like I said, she was poetic, spiritual. Vulnerable actually. Even more tuned in to unreality I reckon, since baby William died from cot death. We tried for another baby – but nothing happened. Our sex life was OK, but no baby. That was a year before Arielle disappeared, the cot death. You know. Naturally the police, once they had decided to take my report of her being missing seriously, wanted to study her emails on my laptop for clues to her 'disappearance'. They didn't find anything particularly useful, I have to say. There were messages to her so-called friend Ginny Peach – just down the road – a forty-minute walk. I will have more to say about Ginny in due course. Obviously. I shot her after all. This is my confession. I need to explain the whys and wherefores of that. It's a pity I have gone blank about the rifle. Where would I put such a thing? As far as I can tell none of my guns is missing. That's an odd thing. I shot her, but what with? And where the hell is it? And I didn't drive down there because the ute was in the shed on blocks, and I would never take Arielle's little Fiesta over that track. I don't even know why I keep the Fiesta really. I guess I still believe she's coming home. I do, yes I do believe that. I know she's out there somewhere. The messages on the laptop were short and fanciful, scattered thoughts about unicorns and things like that. I don't know. Ginny's an artist – was an artist – more later – she did pictures of fantasy creatures. I think she actually believed in them. Arielle did too. Unicorns were real to her. It sometimes seemed to me that Ginny sort of led her on a bit, you know. Owls and unicorns and hares. People have said Ginny was a kind of witch. I don't believe in that stuff, but she was – well, strange. Was Arielle depressed, what with the cot death and everything, the police said. I had to say I didn't really know. The policewoman gave me a funny look when I said it. Well, with Arielle, you couldn't really tell about a thing like that. I was teaching her how to shoot, to take her mind off things. She wasn't bad, actually. They took the laptop away, said there might be clues in the emails, or in websites she might have visited. Social media they said. Arielle didn't do any social media. They brought it back after about three weeks. Said there was nothing there. They would have read my emails too, of course. Well, they wouldn't get much out of orders for seeds and fertiliser, and parts for the generator. I looked at Arielle's emails – there were four that mentioned something that happened when Arielle was out walking in the mornings. And answers from Ginny too. I suppose the police kept a file of all that. I certainly didn't keep any of it. They say things live forever in cyberspace, even on the laptop itself. Like ghosts and spirits. Floating around and coming back to haunt you. I don't know how to get them back, but maybe the police do. They did tell a story, those emails. I wish I had the exact words now. But anyhow, the story was this, more or less. One morning when Arielle was walking on the path through the scrub round the back of the Starlight, she saw up ahead a big animal in the middle of the path, at the bend. She thought it would run off, but it stood there, staring straight at her. It was a hare, an enormous big buck hare. She stood absolutely still. The hare stood still. Like a kind of standoff I think. There was an eerie silence. She couldn't stand there forever, so she moved very slowly closer and closer, but the hare didn't move. She wasn't frightened for some reason. Arielle went past it, kept going slowly and quietly, and when she turned round, a few metres down the track, the hare was gone. She told me about this and I thought it was probably her imagination, but I didn't say so. You didn't say things like that to Arielle. I went along with it. You could say I was humouring her. Of course she emailed Ginny who came right back with her usual rot. I think Ginny believed the hare was real, and she went on about how it's this symbol of fertility, and how it was giving Arielle a message – Arielle would soon have another baby. Arielle told me this – she was breathless with excitement. And I have to say she was extra loving in the bedroom afterwards. So I reckon I can thank Ginny for that at least. But then, about three weeks later, it happened again – Arielle met the hare at the bend in the path, and they stood and stared at each other – Arielle said they communed – for a very long time, a really really long time, like twenty minutes she said. Well you never heard of a hare sitting still for twenty minutes did you? There was a strange white light. Then the hare nodded, and she knew she was meant to move on, and she did, and when she looked back it was gone. When she told me I really started to get worried and I thought maybe I should take her to the doctor or something. But what would I say. What kind of an idiot would I look, telling dithering bloody Barry Smith that my wife was seeing visions? He'd put her on pills I reckon, and turn her into a real zombie. So I let it go. But Ginny Peach didn't let it go. Oh no. No way. Ginny was beside herself with excitement, and I vividly remember reading her emails (after Arielle had disappeared – I didn't read them before – I'm quite strict about things like that) where she said the thing to do to 'respond to the visitation' was to get me to go out round Moonlight Flat or somewhere far enough away and shoot a hare and 'apply the ears' to the soles of Arielle's feet. And before sleep we were to *bathe her face in the blood*. In the morning we were supposed to wash her face with strawberry juice and cowslip water. Then she would definitely conceive. Cowslip water? Arielle told me this and I rang Ginny and said she had to stop the bullshit for God's sake. It was driving Arielle round the bend. She could tell I meant it, and she said she would lay off. She was only trying to help. Yeah. Trying to help. Then she sent Arielle an email saying the creature would appear for a third time, and it would speak. Arielle must on no account reply, she was just supposed to listen, take instruction. It was dangerous to speak to a haunting sacred hare. You could quite easily be carried off beyond the shades. When Arielle disappeared Ginny actually came round here and started raving about the abduction, and I sent her packing. Told her never to come back here. Ever. And she never did. But she talked, and I heard some of the talk, and what she said was that one day Arielle would return, in some kind of spirit form, and she would commit an act of sacrifice. Well when I saw those paintings of the hares, and those creepy portraits of Arielle dissolving into the landscape, I somehow knew what I had to do. I should never have gone to the bloody opening in the first place. I don't really like art, but I was trying to be agreeable. Anyhow I knew I had to go home after the opening and get a rifle and finish off the witch. I mean bitch. And I did. That's the truth, the whole truth, and nothing but the truth. I can't explain about the gun. I can't explain about how I got from my house to hers and back again – but I think I must have walked. Maybe I ran. I just remember seeing all those bloody pictures of great big hares, and Arielle a thing in the background, and I saw red, and I killed Ginny Peach. She had it coming. The End.

Coda

But it was not the end. Three weeks after the shooting a surveyor doing work for a wind farm collective down on Moonlight Flat found, in a remote and ruined stone cottage, the skeleton of a woman. Pure chance. When it was established that these were the remains of Arielle, the mysteries of it all only deepened. She had died as the result of a blow to the head. No weapon. No clues? Was Dan Tasco a slow and deliberate serial killer of some weird and wonderful kind? If he killed Ginny because Ginny knew he had killed Arielle and left her out at Moonlight, why did he confess to shooting Ginny, and not to killing Arielle? If Ginny knew where Arielle was, why didn't she say? He could never really explain why he would kill Ginny anyway. (And for that matter, it was never clear why he would kill Arielle.) I think I said there were interlocking mysteries here. Something came over him, he was not himself. He had to shoot Ginny. He must have been compelled to do it. Did he suddenly discover that Ginny had killed Arielle all those years ago? Why would she do that? And if she did, why not report her to the police? Elizabeth McGee could prove on points of circumstance that Dan did not kill Ginny. It's a pity to end up with so many questions. But all I can really tell you is that Dan didn't go to trial; after a time he simply went back to his sunflowers. Fields and rivers of pure gold. A photographer turned some pictures of it into postcards. There was a running hare in one of them. He swore it wasn't there when he took the picture. So far the building of the wind farm is in doubt. And out at Moonlight Flat people say there is quite an unusual infestation of hares.

ON THE MOUNTAINS OF THE MOON

I've had occasion recently to think a lot about Queenstown. I've never been there, never been to the west coast of Tasmania at all. I believe Queenstown is very beautiful, in its way. It's a mining settlement named after Queen Victoria in 1897. They discovered gold there. It's always gold, isn't it? I thought I'd google, although I realise you can't believe everything you're told on google. The headings that came up were, in order: Accommodation; Weather; Attractions; Caravan Park. I think I knew about the weather – wet, often very wet. People do a roaring trade in umbrellas. My mother told me that once. There's an art deco theatre, the Paragon, built in 1932, now restored and used for movies and 'events'. It's one of the attractions. I must say it looks handsome on my screen. I have a cousin called Marjory who lived in Queenstown, and she used to play the piano and sing at the Paragon. She sometimes stayed with my family at Evandale, and she'd entertain us with her very pretty soprano 'I heard a robin singing'. I know the degraded landscape surrounding Queenstown resembles the mountains of the moon, and is therefore surreal and breathtaking. But, as I say, I've never actually been to Queenstown. So what I say here is second-hand.

When we lived at Evandale (a hop, skip and jump from the Launceston airport) there were two families called the Pilgrims and the Princes. Judith and Julian Pilgrim. Mary-Ann, Kay, Sandra, Tony and Paul Pilgrim. Mrs Pilgrim was Mrs Prince's sister. I used to play with the Prince and Pilgrim children, in the bush, down the creek, in and out of back yards. And sometimes we held mock funerals and weddings behind St Mary's (oldest timber Catholic church in the South Pacific – you can see I'm quoting google again – I never knew this at the time). The church is now deconsecrated and I think it's used as a house. I can't really imagine living in it. Julian Pilgrim was always the priest in our games; Tony Prince (we didn't even think about the meaning of his name, actually) was the bridegroom; sometimes I was the bride and sometimes the bridesmaid, depending on the whims of Judith Pilgrim and all the Prince girls. There were various other boys and girls who came and went. Then there were the funerals. Again Julian was the priest, and we took it in turns to be the corpse and the weeping mourners. The corpse was a good role. At the time. Once Tony said he wanted to be the priest and so Julian said he would be the corpse. He was the funniest body we had ever had, rolling his eyes and baring his teeth and then jumping up and chasing Tony around the paddock. (Well, you had to be there.) When Marjory was with us she would sing 'Ave Maria'. I make it all sound good fun and peaceful enough, but in fact we often fought and bickered – and bit each other. Biting and punching and kicking were the thing. That was all once upon a time – or as Julian now often says: 'Erase una vez'. He also says the bit that comes at the end of the fairy tale, the happily ever after: 'Reniaron en su pais y, si no se han muerto, viviran todavia.' You could say he's a bit affected, but really the phrases come to him quite naturally. I copied them out of an email – hope I got them right.

Julian studied literature and languages, and for many years he has taught Australian Literature at the university in Barcelona. I've visited him there, and sometimes he comes to stay with me and my husband Tom in Adelaide. I have always loved Julian. His life partner is Javier, an art dealer. They live in an amazing apartment where you can hardly move for paintings and sculptures and so on. It's art nouveau, the apartment, but the artworks come from all sorts of historical periods.

Marjory married a man from Philadelphia and as I say, I haven't heard from her for years. I recently heard the 'robin singing' song on the radio, and it took me back. Tony is the only one who still lives in Evandale; he and his wife run a fancy inn, the Fox and Hounds, on the road to Launceston. It's hard to imagine Tony being hospitable. In my old picture book there's a drawing of children asleep in the bed of the giant, and the giant is standing over them with a big knife. That's my idea of landlord Tony. His mother used to say – Oh, Tony, he's always up to mischief, that boy.

Of course I never hear from him. Heavens, of course not! Looking back, I realise I didn't like him at all, ever. Obviously. But you played with whoever was around. He was one of the Princes, so he was part of the games. He was the most violent one, angry and often out of control. And at one of our weddings behind the church he once peed in my face. I probably shouldn't say it, but one of the MacArthur boys, Joey, was accidently shot and killed when they were all out rabbiting, and I reckoned it was Tony pulled the trigger. Nothing was ever proved. He liked to play tricks on people too – like hiding behind the hedge and jumping out at you waving his father's old sword. It's all so long ago it's like a story or another life, from the perspective of today. Strange to say, Tony married the dead boy's sister. Or is it strange; I don't know. I'm pretty sure now that Joey was gay, but that never crossed my mind – it was beyond my understanding – at the time. Although when Tony was in his twenties I saw him beat up Ralphie Best outside the local garage, telling him to stay away from Tony's young brother Paul. And somebody told me he signed a petition to get rid of the gay minister at the Methodist Church – not that he was remotely interested in the Methodist Church or any church for that matter.

I was surprised when the letter came from Marjory in Philadelphia. As I said, I haven't heard from her for years, until now that is. When she got to the point in the letter, after the niceties, she said she had just heard that Julian Pilgrim died in 1990, and asked me, sounding hurt, why I hadn't told her. She put her email on the letter, so I emailed her. It turns out she was playing around on the internet, putting in the names of people she used to know, and she found a thing that said Julian had died, in 1990, in Queenstown Tasmania. It had the names of his parents and his sister, the dates and places of his parents' births and deaths, the date of Judith's birth, 1940. I went to the site, and sure enough, there it was: Julian Francis Pilgrim b.1936 Evandale, Tasmania, d.1990 Queenstown, Tasmania. Queenstown, why Queenstown? That's when I started looking at the Queenstown sites. Not that they told me anything I needed to know of course. I'd never seen a picture of the Paragon Theatre before – that was nice. I reminded Marjory of how she used to sing there, and she said heavens she had almost forgotten. We talked about the old days behind St Mary's and she told me she used to be really scared of Tony.

I wondered about telling Julian. The internet is awash with lies. Does it matter? In the end I did tell him, and he just treated it as a joke. 'Requiescat in pace. Happily ever after, if he hasn't died on us in Queenstown,' he said. I said why Queenstown, and he said he supposed it was because he's gay. I don't know how you find out who posts such things on the internet. It must be possible to work it out, mustn't it? Everybody says I'm making a fuss about nothing. But I don't think it's nothing. I hate it, simply hate it. And it means that somebody hates Julian, a lot. I ask myself who would want Julian dead. In Queenstown. On the mountains of the moon. Possibly a number of people I have never heard of. But I have to tell you – you have guessed already of course – my number one suspect is Tony. I'm definitely pointing the finger at Tony Prince, host of the Fox and Hounds. I don't think I have to be psychic to see it, and one day I might work out how to prove it. He'd think it was funny, saying Julian died in Queenstown, like pissing in your face I suppose. But in the meantime I think Tom and I might just take a little holiday in Queenstown which has captured my imagination. We'll go to the movies at the Paragon; drive out and gaze at the mountains of the moon. Take an umbrella. Not that any of this will get me any closer to the truth about the internet thing. Julian says I must send him a postcard; the old post office in Orr Street is a very handsome Victorian building, likewise the Empire Hotel – if I can believe the images on my screen. What *can* you believe, really, what can you believe?

NO THROUGH ROAD

In 1990, $6000 (Australian) was a fair bit to pay for a raincoat by any standards. Margot was never able to establish that this is what her daughter Pamela really did. All she had to go on was information in a letter from Pamela's eight-year-old daughter. Perhaps the child meant $600.

This is, however, unlikely, since Pamela was at the time spending with considerable abandon a legacy from her late aunt, was separated from her husband, and was living in sin in Paris with a charming Austrian named Klaus. The child, Chloë, had a French nanny named Sidi, and seemed to all intents and purposes to be growing up as a little French mademoiselle. She had her frocks and coats made by a dressmaker, and she resembled the solemn child of a European aristocrat. Possibly not entirely a bad thing. Klaus was some kind of minor royalty from somewhere, and Pamela was developing the habit of shopping at the fashion houses, going to openings and shows, the ballet, the opera, and very very smart parties.

In 1992, in hindsight, Margot felt that she had had a premonition, had seen the writing on the wall, had known that Klaus was going to run off with Sidi. And she was right. This seemed to leave Pamela and Chloë high and dry (with at least one very expensive raincoat) in a rather nice apartment in the sixteenth. Pamela took a job (!) as a translator with the Australian embassy and began a relationship (as it was called) with Noah Prendergast, a rising diplomatic star. Perhaps he was a come-down after the noble foreign rat Klaus von Something-or-other, but a good thing about it all was that Noah's Melbourne family lived only two streets away from Margot (and Pamela's father Walter) in the haven of the wealthy suburb of Toorak. So there was a certain sigh of relief over the breakfast table in Yarra Close (No Through Road, Local Traffic Only). Pamela and Noah had been to the same parties, had even, in some long lost teenage moment, spent a night of youthful passion in a comfy Toorak tree-house at the bottom of Winsie Hopetoun's family garden. Winsie herself is a not insignificant character in this tale. It was she who married Pamela's ex-husband, father of Chloë, after the divorce in 1991. This divorce left Pamela free to marry Klaus, or, as it happened, Noah.

Yes, there is something pleasantly circular about it all, some-thing nice and neat and satisfying. One of Winsie's cousins married Pamela's elder brother and they went to live in the US. Yes it was all neat enough. At least on the surface. And the dramas, tears, celebrations and resolutions gave the old set, the men and women who had mingled as teenagers at those tree-house, pool, ski, sailing and tennis parties long ago, plenty of material to consider.

Here and now, as I tell the tale in 2010, the major players are still going strong.

Margot and Walter (retired from the Bench) are pretty ancient, but still happily ensconced in their old mock Tudor house, still surrounded by lovely English gardens with gently sloping lawns and a series of lily ponds through which gurgles an artificial stream. It is understood that in this time of severe water shortage the water that descends and babbles through the ponds is just the same old ingenious water over and over again. The housekeeper, Mrs Dwyer, who has been with them for nearly forty years, is almost as old as Margot and Walter, but she soldiers on, an integral part of the household, keeping things up to scratch, keeping everything ticking away.

Pamela and Noah are still married (everyone remains astonished, reserving final judgement, watching and waiting) and have two children. Noah abandoned the diplomatic world for the academic, and Pamela became of all things a partner in a fancy publishing house specialising in gorgeous coffee table books about art and fashion and food and so forth. Pamela and the books are glossy and much prized.

Winsie and Pamela's ex have parted, but not before producing a couple of children who move in the same circles as the two fresh children of Pamela and Noah. The fate of Sidi and Klaus is unknown or at least obscure – they have slipped into that lovely European twilight zone of money and minor aristocracy invented once upon a time by Henry James, and brought to mind (oh déjà-vu!) by the screenplays of Merchant Ivory.

Chloë is twenty-eight. Twenty-eight!

So where has Chloë been all this time, and what has she been doing, and where is that lonely little girl who wrote the letter to her grandmother, the letter containing the startling information about the price of the raincoat, and also the intelligence that at night she could see in the distance the Eiffel Tower? It was a poignant fact that she would 'watch the lights' on the Eiffel Tower as they were turned off some time in the early hours. 'Mum bought a raincoat. It cost $6000. It's grey. At night I watch the lights go out on the Eiffel Tower. I miss you. Please send my velveteen rabbit.' Margot, unable to locate the rabbit in question, duly purchased a new one and sent it on to Chloë who wept at its brand new fresh texture and smell and the set of extra clothes for it to wear on outings, so Margot said, in the Bois de Boulogne. To her grandmother Chloë wrote: 'Thank you very very much for sending me the rabbit. He is lovely. It is fun to change his clothes. I miss you very much.' Do I need to tell you that Chloë left the rabbit behind one day on a chair at the Grand Guignol in the Luxembourg Gardens? Such things are written, meant to be. The child did not weep over the loss. Some other child no doubt smiled with glee at its own good fortune. The extra suit of clothes was given to a tartan bear which looked quite handsome in them, and was remarked upon by people in the play area of the Parc Monceau.

Chloë's French is truly excellent. When she left school she studied art and design in Melbourne, and at some incredibly young age set up her own fashion label, CDM (Chloë Dans le Métro) and became a household word. Movie stars and singers and royals and the wives of sportsmen stepped out of limos and onto red carpets wearing CDM. She is celebrated as a brilliant, an *inspired* cutter. Her logo, in a gesture to that old lost velveteen rabbit, is the silver profile of the hare on the defunct Irish three-penny bit, confusing rabbits with hares. She generally gives her creations names, and yes there is a Sidi in one of the collections, and as it happens it is a gun-metal coloured silky opera coat, able to double as – you guessed it – a raincoat. And yes the price tag is $6000. Nobody bats an eyelid at the price, although several people have expressed surprise at the utilitarian possibility of the thing. Raincoat.

Somebody bought it and took it to England (so light to pack, so elegant, so *grey*, so vast and so amusingly shroud-like) where it was worn by an Australian student at Oxford who drowned in a drunken boating accident so that the coat became part of a forensic exhibit as seen on TV in shows such as *Silent Witness*. It was suggested that if the student had not been hampered by the voluminous complicated billowing nature of the coat she probably would not have drowned. Much was made of the fact that the girl had been completely naked under the coat. It is strange really how a kind of stuffy conservative morality leaps forward when nakedness and accident appear to conspire to form a recipe for fatality. At some time before dawn the girl, with a blood alcohol reading of .06, had slipped from the rowdy deck where undergraduate revellers revelled and caroused and capered unaware of the silent thing that was happening, the thing that would haunt them all for the rest of their lives.

Until the garment came to grisly prominence, Margot had been unaware of its existence. But when Chloë's label was named in a news item, and the coat was displayed as it had appeared on a catwalk in Paris, Margot's sharp eye, ear and mind registered something sad regarding her successful little granddaughter.

The price tag, said the newsreader, was said to be in the vicinity of $6000. People gasped in amazed and eager horror. Imagine. And the girl was naked. It was like something out of the nineteen twenties. Margot invited Chloë round to Yarra Close for afternoon tea in the sunny little conservatory off the library. 'Just the two of us Chloë – it has been some time since we had a nice chat.' The friendly brown English teapot – Margot is in fact known for being severely unpretentious in the matter of her teapot – it once belonged to her mother. Yet she uses Clarice Cliff 'Sundew' cups as a matter of course. Mrs Dwyer's trusty shortbread. Whitework linen napkins embroidered by Margot's mother in an age long past and gone. A bowl of bright nasturtiums, droplets of water glittering in the hearts of the broad circular leaves.

The young woman and her grandmother talked joyfully and quietly about the everyday, the marvellous success of CDM, the fashion colours for the coming season, the recent birth of another great-grandchild in of all places New Mexico. As was her custom on such cosy occasions, Margot gave Chloë the choice of some nice pieces of jewellery from her collection. This time Chloë chose a pair of silver Victorian mourning earrings set with lozenges of black glass that was subtly etched with the design of a swallow in flight. A very good choice. So charming, flattering, unique. And to the gift of the earrings Margot added a bundle of Chloë's own childhood drawings and little stories and letters. 'You might like to have these.' Among the letters was the raincoat one from Paris, but it was not discussed. It was really just one among many letters, but in Margot's heart that letter, and the dreadful story of the young woman in Oxford, was evidence of something sad and unresolved in her granddaughter's damaged spirit. Would Chloë look at the drawings, read the stories, the letters? Did *she* connect her own unhappy life as a little girl in Paris with the event in Oxford? Perhaps not. Margot didn't know, and would probably never know. But she considered that the best place for the Paris letter in particular was among Chloë's own papers. Or in her own rubbish bin. That was the way Margot did things, she gave the opportunity and then let things take their own course. It had always worked, or so Margot thought. The new season's colours were going to be celadon and light lilac. With masses of heavy silver jewellery. Walter came in from the garden and had a cup of strong tea with Margot and Chloë who was wearing the earrings. 'Gran gave me all these old drawings. Look at this! A picture of you Papa standing in the rain with your wig on. What big ears you have. And here's Mum and Dad both look-ing like horses. I remember that. Look at all these letters Papa. Fancy keeping them. Gran you're so sentimental.' Chloë and Walter were laughing. Margot seemed more subdued. Walter said, 'See, it was always obvious you were a born artist.' With the pictures and stories and letters in a brown paper carry-bag Chloë left in a breathless rush, as always. 'Bye Gran! Bye Papa! Must rush. Stay beautiful.'

Margot sent a wreath to the funeral in Oxford. She was unknown to the family of the dead girl, but she signed her name and gave her address. The family naturally assumed their loved one had somehow known a Mrs Margot Bloch of Yarra Close, Toorak, Australia. In due course Margot received a card of thanks for her kindness and her thoughtfulness.

<h1 style="text-align:center">THINK OF ME</h1>

I was feeling good, better than good, wonderful. Flying to Hobart to start a new life with Ben. Like a barn swallow coming south for the winter. I met Ben at my sister's wedding in Sydney – very auspicious – and now here I was, joyfully stashing my backpack under the seat in front, heading for a new marriage and even a new job in Ben's brother's law office. Yes, it was like a dream come true. He was forty-five and never married, I was forty, divorced, no children.

I helped her with her bag. Swung it up into the luggage compartment. She was a small woman probably in her seventies, wearing those sensible dreary clothes, navy and grey with incredibly expensive sneakers, that such women often seem to wear for travelling. Her perfume was also expensive – I couldn't quite place it – but of course it's always a relief on an aircraft to sit beside somebody who smells nice.

We took off, and I took out my Kindle and started reading *The Catcher in the Rye* which I had always meant to read, and never had. She sat with her small delicate hands folded in her lap, staring straight ahead. We were not really quite ignoring each other, seemed to be silent companions, not altogether strangers. Sometimes we spoke. She said she was thinking of getting a Kindle, and was it really good? I was not concentrating on my reading, not concentrating on my nice neighbour – I was really sealed in a bubble of happy anticipation, the image of Ben and me in the tub, at the spa where we had spent our last night together in the Blue Mountains, occupying my whole consciousness. Then she broke the spell.

'So what takes you to Hobart?' she said. Clunk.

'Oh – I – I'm meeting my fiancé. We're getting married soon.'

She lifted her hands almost as if in prayer, and smiled at me. Was I supposed to ask her why she was going there? I thought so.

'Ah,' she was suddenly grave and somehow soft, 'ah – I am on my way to the funeral of my son and daughter-in-law.' The expression on her face had barely changed, she seemed to have a permanent little smile, although now I more than half faced her I could see her eyes were steady with pain.

This statement was made quietly, almost apologetically. I responded with the usual helpless words: I'm so sorry.

The silence that fell between us then was terrible. Desperately I searched for something more to fill the void. All I said, in a stupid thick sort of voice was: That is very sad.

Then I was sorry I'd said such a dumb thing. But what can you say? And how could she just sit there on the aircraft so composed and sweet-smelling and twinkly and normal? Should I ask her if she wants to talk about it? It was not my business. Images of car crashes, drownings, suicides, murders – airline crashes – all flashed through my mind. The bubble of happiness in the spa had broken. I was now drawn into her world, her sorrow. How to proceed from here?

'They must have been very young?' I ventured.

'Mmm, he was nearly forty. She was too. Both. So young.'

I didn't have to ask any more questions, the story she wanted and did not want to tell was already on its way.

'There are two little children. I am bringing them back to Sydney with me afterwards. Alice-May, that was their mother, died in the accident you see.'

It was as if I was supposed to know about the accident.

'I feel I know the children well, we have had many visits, and we've talked on Skype since they were babies. Cooper and Sunday. Their other grandparents are in Japan, very old, too old. In Sydney they will have their cousins. Nearby.'

She went into a little moment of silence as if she were hopefully contemplating the happiness that was in store for the two orphans.

'Robert worked as a doctor on the ships that go to Antarctica. Ever since he was a little boy he loved Antarctica – the ice, the bird life – I don't know – just the strangeness of that world far to the south of everything. Alice-May was an artist, photographer. You might know her pictures of Antarctica. Robert met her on one of the boats. Her parents can't even come to the funeral. Her father is very ill. It is so sad.'

She was beginning to weep. I said nothing. Then suddenly she rallied and said,

'We are sending half of the ashes to Japan. Both. Half will come back to Sydney.'

I had begun to feel that I had too intimate a knowledge of all this. I actually wished I knew what form the accident had taken, but naturally was unable to ask. Were they lost on the ice? I have never heard of people being lost on the ice these days. In my mind I settled for a car accident, such things being so very common.

Then she took from her wallet a photograph of the couple and the children, all so beautiful, smiling under the Christmas tree. She was composed again, almost as if showing me an ordinary picture in the ordinary way.

'They are very beautiful,' I said, feeling like an idiot. 'Such lovely children.'

The little girl was about seven, and something strangely familiar shone out of her features, which were more Japanese than Australian, her mother being, I realised, fully Japanese. The name Alice-May – maybe it was a common name for Japanese girls in Australia. And then I remembered. Alice-May Nakamol was a girl in my dorm at boarding school. Did I read in the old collegians' magazine that she had married somebody? If I knew the name of my flying companion it might mean something to me. I tried to look at the woman's boarding pass that was poking up out of the seat pocket. No luck. Then she got up to go to the toilet and I quickly flicked it out. Jean Paton. Robert Paton? I was suddenly convinced that Alice-May Nakamol had married Robert Paton. But I had to be sure.

When Jean came back I lied, 'Your daughter-in-law – I think I have seen some of her photographs. Was she Alice-May Nakamol?'

'Yes, she said,' quite animated suddenly, 'yes, that was her maiden name. She always used it professionally.

'Ah,' I said, 'her pictures are really wonderful.'

The aircraft was beginning its descent into Hobart. My mind was now racing with scattered recollections of Alice-May. How she had never had a pet, except, she said, once a paper fish.

How she sang like an angel. How she cried every night for her family and her beloved best friend Akako. And then I remembered the little box she gave me for my birthday. It was a tiny wooden thing, the size of a matchbox, maybe, and on the lid was pasted a strip of paper on which was some Japanese writing. I asked her what it said, and she told me: Think Of Me. Inside was a photograph of Alice-May. Somewhere in a trunk in my mother's house, that little box lay sleeping with other assorted treasures from my schooldays. Think Of Me.

There was now no time, no way I could somehow cut across the woman's grief with the news of the fragile connection between us. I felt helpless and almost overwhelmed with grief of my own.

We landed with a bump. Eventually I handed Jean her bag from the overhead locker.

'Goodbye,' I said. 'I am so very sorry.'

She smiled her composed sweet smile, straightened her back, and made her way across the short and shimmering tarmac. I watched her through a window as she walked, slow but determined. I remained in a bottleneck in the aircraft until long after she had gone. Eventually I too crossed the tarmac. There was my adorable Ben, so present and alive and waiting for me with his arms wide. I ran. I fell into his arms, and, in the confusion of emotions that were coursing through me, I began to shake and sob.

'Hey, Sal, Sal, what is it? Has something happened?'

'Oh, Ben, it's so incredible to see you. Just so good to see you.'

'You too, Sal. You too. Let's go home. Cheer up. We're going home.'

'Yes. Yes we are.'

I think I was recovering, but the memory of Alice-May's little face in the Japanese box was haunting me.

As we passed through the terminal, I saw a rack of postcards, and I stopped. Leaping out at me was a glorious photograph of Antarctic ice. By Alice-May Nakamol. I bought one for myself and one for Ben. On the back of his I wrote: Think Of Me. He looked at me for quite a long time with his quizzical smile.

THE LEGACY OF RITA MARQUAND

The first Rita Marquand oil painting I ever saw was at a garage sale on the sloping lawn of a huge old house in Tasmania a couple of years ago. Ever since I was a girl at art school I have been collecting the works of lesser known and unknown Australian women painters. The collection is now quite extensive. Rita's picture was on a smallish piece of plywood, framed in an elaborate chipped gilt frame – two young girls in filmy white dresses playing among yellow grass. The grass is alive with subtle colours, the girls caught in a moment of intimate laughter. It was titled and signed on the back in red pen – 'The Deedees' Rita Marquand, Fatima, 1927. I bought the painting in 2000 for two dollars from a man who said it had been done by a distant relative of his late wife. This is a typical story from my files – the discovery of a new 'unknown' woman painter who sets me off on a journey into the poignant past. There was so much talent, passion, beauty locked away in the lives of women before the liberation of the seventies came along and gave girls the chance to show what they are made of.

This journey led me from Launceston to Devonport, to Blackwood Creek, to Hobart, and finally to the Huon Valley where I found at last the house called 'Fatima' in which Rita Marquand had lived and painted. Along the way, I was able to collect five other pictures that had somehow been preserved – one was a glowing image of a blindfolded angel standing sorrowfully beside a burnt-out gum tree. There was a strangeness to Rita's work that fascinated me, a strangeness that I do not often encounter in the paintings of my unknown women, most of whom paint fairly simple landscapes, gardens, houses. I get pictures from op shops and skips and cellars and attics – and sometimes from kitchen shelves where they have been for two or three generations.

By the time I tracked Rita down to 'Fatima' I was very interested not only in her paintings but also in the story of the lives of the two girls in 'The Deedees'. With her large family and a small farm to manage, it is a miracle Rita ever put brush to canvas. But this is something I have discovered about my women painters, they kept their sanity by snatching moments of creative passion from the hours of duty and family responsibility.

I discovered that Dymphna and Dolores were sisters, born at 'Fatima' in a small rural town in the Huon Valley. I have pieced together as best I can the story of what happened to them. I have taken the liberties of a storyteller at times, trying to imagine how people must have felt, how they must have thought about things. Some of the material I found in small diaries that Dymphna kept over the years. These were often illustrated, showing that Dymphna had inherited her mother's talent. However, I never saw a finished work by Dymphna. Between the pages of the diaries I found old letters and cards from Dolores to Dymphna, and one pale blue love letter to Dolores from a man called Geoffrey (My Sweetest Angel, Dolly…). The girls had two older brothers, a baby sister and baby brother, Sissy and Jo-Jo. The place was described as a dairy farm but, in fact, it was a small property where the Marquands kept some cows, grew some apples and kept their heads above water.

Everyone on the farm – Rita, her husband Paul, and all the children – worked hard: up before daybreak, finishing long after dark. I sat in Rita's old kitchen, at the table where she had made the bread for the family, and I listened to Margaret, the young wife of another Jo-Jo, Rita's grandson. Her baby crawled around on the wooden floor where Dymphna and Dolores must have crawled. Born in 2005, he is the only descendant so far of Rita and Paul in this generation. The older boys died in the Second World War and Sissy never had children. Margaret and Jo-Jo were amazed that anybody would be interested in Rita's paintings.

Dymphna was named for an aunt who was named for the patron saint of the mentally ill (or, as they said in the thirties, the insane). Dolores was named for the very sad aspect of the Virgin Mary. The names turned out to be, I am sorry to say, prophetic. The two girls were known as the Deedees.

They were inseparable. Dolores (Dolly) was eighteen months older than Dymphna. Dolly was very bright and pretty, with softly curling brown hair, and Dymphna (Dimples) had, as it happened, a dinky little dimpled smile, and hair 'as straight as a packet of candles'. When in the bath, with her stringy hair wet and stuck across her forehead in strands and down her back in damp ribbons, her mother said she was just a dying duck in a thunderstorm.

Apart from their connection with the painting, the lives of Dymphna and Dolores are now of a certain historic interest as they illuminate a past that exercises a fascination in the present. Television is larded with programs where innocent people are forced to relive the lives and times of girls like the Deedees, struggling with the lack of conditioner for their hair, eating bread and dripping (which is the fat that is saved in the baking dish after meat has been roasted). These programs generally emphasise the terrible difficulties of past lives. What I will tell you about the early lives of the Deedees will probably seem impossibly romantic, with a hint of paradise, in spite of what I have said about their being up before dawn.

So, on the Marquands' dairy farm they blossomed. In the spring, apple trees, cherries, plums and almonds, too, turned the hillside into a frothy springtime snow leading down to the river. Note what I said about paradise. Snow, they always called it snow, as they ran, children on legs like elves' legs, across the long grass where the red sorrel grew, wild and rough underfoot, knee-high, and they rolled over and over down the hill. Over and over and over. And then, in the summer, they picked the plums for jam and bottling and harvested the almonds to stir into the dark damp Christmas cakes and the pobbly puddings that hung for months in their calico cloths in the dairy. The girls pelted like the wind, the wind in their hair and in their eyes, danced down the hillside, falling and rolling, tumbling under the almond trees, pastel cotton dresses made by their mother at midnight , skirts flying up, pink pants rude and visible, bare feet hot and lovely, and they lay there, the dappled shadows of the leaves flittering across their faces, faces flushed and glowing. They dangled cherries from their ears. Laughter twittering up into the blossom trees, coin spots of sunlight glimmering across them. Well, was it paradise or wasn't it? This is what Rita captured in 'The Deedees'.

The future was wonderful then. The Deedees were living and laughing – with potatoes and sausages to eat and milk to drink – and fruit – while around them was the Depression. They were in the Depression but they did not know it. They knew a copper full of boiling sheets seething in soap, sheets rinsed in blue from the bluebag, flapping on the clothesline in the sun. Running in and out diving through the flapping sheets, that were sewn down the middle with a heavy seam because they had been split and 'turned' to make them last longer. Their beds were high – tall maple ends with curved edges and a raised wreath of leaves like a medallion in the centre. These were grand old beds from their mother's old home. They called them the American beds, I am not sure why, but maybe they associated them with faraway luxury. They gleamed golden by candlelight. When I came to 'Fatima' and saw the beds they were still beautiful, although the surface of the varnish was now dulled. A child had written her name on one of the bedheads – 'Sissy Marquand slept here' – and somebody had tried to clean it off. But the room, now a guest room, was, Margaret said, much as it had been when the Deedees lived there in the thirties.

Above Dymphna's bed was the traditional picture of the Immaculate Heart. If you are looking for sentimental horror, this is it – the sweetly peachy smiling woman (sad) with her greenish blue cloak and her crown of rosebuds. But then, in her hands, surrounded by a wreath of thorny roses is her heart, which radiates pink and gold light and is surmounted by a hot red flickering flame. This picture would not have been seen as strange by the children. It was the normal image to hang above a bed, but if you think about it, it is really most peculiar. Then, on the wall, over Dolores's bed, hung what I thought was a print of a work of art – 'Madonna of the Goldfinch' by Tiepolo. But, lucky for me, Margaret drew my attention to it, saying, 'Rita did that. She used to copy things, apparently. I think it's so ugly, but we keep it because Rita did it. It's not original – we haven't got any originals – but I suppose it has sentimental value, you know, because she did it. Once there was a print of the painting by Tiepolo hanging there.' This is not the only masterpiece I have found reproduced by one of my women – Georgia James used to do excellent copies of Goya – but it added an exciting new dimension to Rita, in my opinion.

Now, I would rather like to rush ahead and tell you what eventually happened to Dymphna and Dolores but, in fact, the pictures over their childhood beds are relevant to the outcome in a strange way, and so I must pause here to think about them. Life, I find, can sometimes be infused with prophecies or at least shadows and foreshadows. And I need to dwell for a moment on the 'Madonna of the Goldfinch' by Rita Marquand, which hangs in the wall of memory above Dolores Marquand's old American bed.

The child Jesus holds the goldfinch firmly in his left hand, tight, a bundle of taffeta bluish feathers with a bobbing scarlet head. The Holy Child is naked – a striking feature of the picture being the deep red bloody highlights on the mouth of the mother, her collar and sleeve, the head of the bird. The mother gazes downward, the child looks straight at the world, at the viewer, his deep blue eyes still, knowing, sad. Startling and sickening is the bruised red luscious cherry of the baby's lips, as if he had sucked on berries or fresh game. The flesh of the mother and child appears to be not so much alive as on the point of corruption. These observations are mine. Similar thoughts just might have crossed the minds of the Deedees, although I doubt it. Yet it is my understanding that the effects of the images above the beds entered the girls' deep imaginations.

Rita told them that long long ago, at the time of the Crucifixion, a goldfinch took a thorn from the crown-borne-crown of Jesus, and the blood from the holy brow went splashing out and landed on the head of the bird. Hence the little bird's scarlet head. Privately, the Deedees liked to puzzle over that story – if the goldfinch didn't get its red head until it pulled the thorn out of the crown on the dark day of the Crucifixion, how was it the baby Jesus was holding a goldfinch with a bright red head? Ours not to reason why, Rita counselled. Apparently, there are about six hundred known paintings of Madonna and child with goldfinch. I don't wish to burden you with a lot of academic detail, but I think it is worth knowing that in 1952, a writer named Jacques Schnier published an essay entitled 'The Symbolic Bird in Medieval and Renaissance Art' and in that essay he says that the goldfinch signifies the mother herself, the mother is the lost object over which the child desires control. The goldfinch also signifies fertility and is associated with Lucina, ancient goddess of childbirth. These somewhat heavy little messages hanging above the American beds at 'Fatima' can be seen to cast an ironic shadow over the lives of the Deedees. I need here to draw attention to the matters of sex before marriage, unplanned pregnancy and abortion – matters that naturally give rise in the modern mind to the question of contraception. Safe contraception was not dreamt of until the sixties and would not even then have been possible for the Catholic Deedees. You can see that to get pregnant before marriage in this family at that time was to go to hell in a handbasket, and you feel the prob-lem looming, dangling like the pictures over the American beds. Who is going to get pregnant, and what is she going to do next?

Well, it was Dolores, the cheerful one with the very sad name. To the delight of the proud family, Dolores went off to

Hobart to study at the Teachers' College. She was to live at the Sacred Heart Hostel, safe and sound with the nuns, the curfew and the Catholic faith. Her mother made her skirts, coats, blouses, dresses. All afternoon and well into the night the sewing machine would be going k-chick-k-chick-k-chick. Dolores would flit about and try things on and her mother, with pins in her mouth, would say, 'Stand still' and 'Hold up your arm' and 'Stop wriggling'. Auntie Bee knitted jumpers and cardigans for Dolly. Sitting by the fire or under the holly hedge her needles singing away tik-woo-tik-woo-tik. Hot-water-bottle covers. Two brown suitcases filled and folded and fluffed up with every-thing including a new silver compact with face powder. She took a small framed picture of Our Lady of Perpetual Succour and also the painting her mother did in the orchard, 'The Deedees'.

When she was in Hobart , Dolores went to dances on Friday nights. She started smoking and drinking and dancing with all kinds of young men. And some not so young. To start with, she was back at the hostel by ten, but then she discovered how to climb in the laundry window after midnight, having bribed another girl to sign her in at ten. She got up on a stage and sang in the After-Dinner Conservatory. She was incredibly pretty and popular. She was on the downward slide. Lying in bed during the holidays, she would tell Dymphna about some of the things she did, and Dymphna was amazed and fascinated and frightened for her sister's immortal soul. She would wonder how safe it was to ride in cars with men you hardly knew.

Dymphna had heard of at least two girls who had been killed when a car ran into a tree and, of course, there lurked, just below the surface, the terror of pregnancy. Girls would some-times disappear for a few months, gone to stay with relatives on the mainland, and then they would come back and stay at home with their families and never marry, scarred for life.

Dolores was kissing and hugging and driving fast into the countryside. At night, she would cuddle in dark cars beside the river. 'But you have to be a virgin dressed in white and pure when you get married,' Dymphna said, and Dolores said, 'Maybe you do.' She looked at her sister sideways from under her hair and she smiled her little winking crooked pink cherry-cherub smile. It was a naughty smile, a smile that Dymphna somehow linked with the smile in a story the nuns had told them – a girl smiles at a man who beckons her to a doorway, and in the doorway he takes her hand, and he rings the bell and the door opens and they go in and are never seen again because it was the doorway to hell.

Then, one day, Dolores told Dymphna she had a real sweetheart, Geoffrey.

'Why don't you tell Mum and bring him home then?'

'He's a Baptist.'

'Have you been to confession?'

'No.'

The answer came swift and defiant, and Dymphna knew there and then that the writing was on the wall and that the whole thing was out of control. To be involved with a Protestant was worse than having sex and getting pregnant. Geoffrey was going to be a lawyer and he was not a very good Baptist, smoking and drinking and dancing as he did. Dolores planned to get him to convert. Surely he would see reason. If his own family's religion mattered so little to him, why couldn't he become a Catholic? But when she lay in his arms on the grass by the river, none of this mattered, and her wicked heart sang for joy and her blood simmered with a hot excitement that sent her conscience off to sleep.

In the window of a smart Hobart shop one day, Dolores saw something so amazing, so desirable, so drenched in beauty that she did not pay for textbooks but bought the thing instead. It was a dress. I think this was maybe the real beginning of the end, spending the textbook money on the dress to go to the Winter Garden Dance with Geoffrey. When Dolores told Dymphna about the dress Dymphna knew in her heart of heart that the bell of the doorway to hell was ringing.

Dymphna's head was spinning and her heart was beating fast with excitement and desire at the thought of the dress and the dance and the money and the man and the non-existent textbooks. This was the true beginning of the locked-up things that Dymphna could never tell anybody, the source of the guilt that was going to poison her life. Catholic girl meets Baptist boy – Juliet and Romeo – until something fatal and inevitable and blindingly terrible occurs, like when a plane flies into a mountain and explodes, killing all on board. Dymphna held the black box, held it in her shadowed and sorrowful heart, and it stilled her blood, stopped her thoughts, right there in the bedroom of the dairy farm in the lovely valley of the Huon.

It was Dymphna who gave up on life at that point, Dymphna who stopped eating, stopped talking. Not altogether, but she did what they called 'going into herself' and she became a joyless wraith out of the reach of her family and friends. People naturally thought she was considering entering the convent and, in fact, she did feel drawn to that life but (and this is so sad and ironic) she knew that she could not, simply because she would have to confess to all she knew, in due course, about her sister, and that was impossible. Somehow she could hold her knowledge back from everyday confession, but if she entered the convent, everything would have to come spilling out. She would have to spew toads of truth in the dark box of the confessional, and Dolores would never forgive her. Nobody would forgive her. Would God forgive her? God was supposed to do that, but who can divine the depths of reasoning of the mind of God? So what it amounts to is that while Dolores was going to hell, Dymphna was beginning to go, quite simply, mad. The poor Marquands and their two lovely daughters who both ended up so tragically. Margaret was very frank about this – she had no problem telling a perfect stranger that Dymphna had gone mad.

Dolores would tell her sister about the things she did with Geoffrey, sometimes in letters, and Dymphna loved getting the cards and letters, the photographs of picnics and warm days at the beach. The secret thrilling wicked sinful parts of the letters were in secret little envelopes inside the leaves of the main letter. Here is a letter from Dolly – and she would read out the main letter at the family dinner table, driving the evil deeper and deeper into her own heart as she read, knowing she was lying. Dolores went to lectures and wrote essays and played the piano in concerts at the hostel. She described in the secret letters the marvellous miraculous dress she had bought with the textbook money. Dymphna wondered if she would ever see this dress.

She did see it. When her mother went to Hobart and brought all Dolly's things back home. It was lying in the suitcase, on top of everything, the last thing Rita had put in. It was wrapped in white tissue paper and Dymphna saw it slide out of its parcel. It slithered onto the white counterpane, underneath Rita's picture of Jesus and his mother and the goldfinch. For some reason, Rita had left the picture of 'The Deedees' at the hostel in Hobart .

They were accustomed enough to deaths in the family – two dead babies, grandparents, an uncle in Egypt in the war, a simple aunt who drifted away from this world – a fish disappearing in an ancient Mongolian stream. But they were not prepared for Dolores, the lovely wild sister.

Dolores had come home on the train from town and had died in a fevered pool of blood in the bedroom. There had never been a death like this one in this family. Dymphna was in a trance of shock, all the details of the sin and the crime flooding into her brain and heart, blocking reason, dashing reality into shards of broken clay.

In the 1930s, sex before marriage, unplanned pregnancy and abortion were highly risky enterprises. Pregnancy was OK in marriage, indeed required, but the other pregnancies were sins, and abortion was, of course, also a crime. If you saw the movie *Vera Drake* you would know all about that. The bedroom curtains, white linen backed with sunlight and flittered with shadows, were drawn against the day, and Dolores lay there dead in the half-dark.

'Dymphna,' Rita said, in a firm, cold, steady voice, 'get your father. Then call the priest and the doctor.'

'Call the priest and the doctor,' she said, in that firm, cold, steady voice. That was the order in which she placed them – first the priest and then the doctor. And that was the way she designated them. Not Father Gayle and Doctor Rush, but the priest and the doctor. First of all, Dymphna got her father from the deep shadows in the pungent darkness of the milking shed. Between the telephone calls to the priest and the doctor and the inky arrival of those specialists in mortality, Rita sent her living daughter to the linen press for clean sheets, to the laundry for water and soap and towels. It was a secret now between the mother and daughter, a secret spelling the death of Dolores and the end of meaning. It was already a dark bond and a smudge of dirty ice between them. What would the doctor make of it? He would know what had happened for sure. And Dr Rush was a Catholic doctor.

Would he describe the matter as being the result of a 'miscarriage'? Death the result of excessive loss of blood. Is that what he would do? To save the Catholic honour of the family. Well, in fact, he could only half save it, since Dolores was not married. Wasn't he bound by law to report the truth? Truth. To discover the name of the person in town who had done this to Dolores, who had opened her up (ripped her open?) and let the baby out and sent her home to die? Wasn't it his duty to see that a judge would send those people, that person, that woman, that witch – to prison? To save other girls from the fate of this glittering fanciful unmarried Dolores who could not believe that this was happening? Dymphna wondered what her mother was thinking of saying to Father Gayle. Perhaps, she thought, my lies have killed my sister, lies that hid the truth she shared with me. The truth that Dolly shared with me like secrets in the white and yellow bedroom long ago, so long ago in the giggling twilight of summer childhood. Perhaps the lies have killed her after all.

'Just lend me ten pounds,' Dolores said, 'and when I come home it will be all over and nobody will know any different.' But Dymphna knew it wasn't going to work like that – they would never get away with it. Ten pounds from her bankbook was a great big sum of money. Dolores sold a coral necklace left to her by Auntie Caroline. Somewhere or other, somehow or other, she sold the necklace. She had a life of mysteries beyond her sister's understanding. How did a girl sell a necklace of darling little antique coral bead strung out in family prayers and unforgotten laughter? And what if their mother got to wondering where it had gone? 'Oh, then I'll say I lost it,' Dolores said, quite solemn, like an actress, she said that. 'I lost it. The clasp was weak. I should have had it attended to, mended. I was saving up to have it mended. Just think – for a little three and sixpence I could have saved Auntie Caroline's coral necklace.'

She smiled. She had a cute pink pixie crooked slightly smile.

Paul came to the bedroom door and Rita went to him. They stood together in a tight embrace, silent, and then they went out to the back door and stood again together, talking, underneath the cherry plum trees. She was explaining, he was listening. He was a silent man, always. He followed his wife's lead in most things, and gynaecology was her province. The blood and the pain and the sometime joy of babies in and out of the womb. Morality was also her area. She had taken on the particular role of wisdom, also practicality.

You could see them, a couple, through the open door, framed in the green doorway, as Dymphna dialled the number for the exchange and asked for the presbytery. Vilma Jones at the exchange would wonder, in her wide-eyed, wide-mouthed, frizzy-haired, blue-dressed way – or perhaps she would know – why Dymphna Marquand was calling the presbytery. Why was she calling? For a blank moment of idiot shock Dymphna suddenly could not remember what this was all about. Then she remembered. When next asked for the doctor's number Vilma knew. The priest and the doctor meant a death. For certain sure. Death or promise of death.

All the time, Dolores was lying on her bed beneath the goldfinch, and the blood was drying, caking, ruby-brown and brilliant, and her father had gone back to the milking shed and Dymphna was arriving in the bedroom with the water and the towels and the clean linen from the sweet lemon linen press. And all the time Rita was firm and cool and clear-headed and coldhearted and hating Dymphna and blaming her. She was guilty, with the black box of truth buried deep inside her heart.

The mother became the priestess at the temple of her dead child and the other child her servant, silent, obedient, afraid, doing everything required except tell the story.

You will have noticed that Geoffrey disappeared a while back. He just went on with his life, occasionally giving a bit of a thought to Dolores Marquand, wondering sometimes what brought on the hush-hush fever that caused the sudden death of this bright and promising young woman. It occurred to me to go on a little treasure hunt, looking for the traces of Geoffrey, but that would be another story altogether.

The priest and the doctor smoothed the way for the sin and the crime to be concealed beneath a convenient felting of lies and half-truths. There was a quiet funeral to which some of the girls from the hostel (their knowing eyes lowered in respect) and two of the nuns (sad faces open as they swallowed the fictions of the fever and the death) came. And the sequinned dress lay forever after in the wooden trunk of fabrics beside the sewing machine. Buried in its coffin, waiting to be cut up into sections, divided into bits, drawn and quartered and reduced to a heap of purple scales. Why was it not destroyed at once? Things old and unwanted or wicked were always being burnt. Was the dress perhaps too strange, too exotic, too desirable, too lovely, too wicked, too powerful? Too mysterious in origin and design, too poisonous? It also obviously held the answer to the question of the death of Dolores. The family could not confront the question, let alone the answer. They prayed every night for the soul of Dolores.

Dymphna went slowly spinning into what they called melancholia, as thin as a rake, as mad a hatter, locked up inside herself, never coming out.

One day, long years after the death of Dolores, Dymphna, who talked and sang a little to herself, opened the camphor-wood trunk. She found two small pink dresses her mother made for them one Christmas Eve, tiny rosebuds printed on the artificial silk, the machine going k-chick-k-chick far into the night, tickling their ears as they wondered what treasures were created, what glamour was being prepared for Christmas Day, hot games under the fruit trees, roly-poly who can roll the fastest to the bottom of the hill. Hair ribbons for church, new and pale pink and silky. Straw hats. A new enormous silky flower on their mother's elegant little navy spotted dress. A handsome family walking with some dignity to church on Christmas Day with new pink dresses k-chick-k-chick. Long, long before the tragedy. Dymphna turned the dresses over in her hands, reverently, and remembered the old cherry plum trees at the back door, how they smelt when they were covered in fruit to be collected, picked and plopped and heaped into large white enamel buckets. They would take the cherry plums around and dish them out to everybody, the priest and the doctor included, and when they came home they would go to bed, and the sewing machine would start up, singing them to sleep. Cream, too, they took gifts of cream from their happy cows to their sometimes happy neighbours. In the milking shed they sang to the cows. 'Bluebird of Happiness', 'Faith of our Fathers', and a song made up by Dolores all about how cows are silly, cows are funny. Dymphna sang that song over to herself as she rifled through the trunk until she came to Dolores's glittering dress. It was what was called a cocktail frock, completely covered in purple sequins, all attached by hand to a black net background, arranged in tight little scales of glitter, in the pattern of the wings of a giant butterfly – shimmering glimmering, with the back so empty and low it dipped right down to the tailbone, and no sleeves, and the front scooping in a swallow dive right down between the breasts. Like a snake it took your breath away, like a quietly singing snake, humming and murmuring and bursting into flames. Royal purple and just a wisp of the wing of a delicate evil insect, so very very beautiful. It lay in the trunk, wounded, defiant, shining, shining through its tears.

'So what do you know about this dress?' Rita had asked.

'I don't know anything about the dress,' Dymphna lied.

Mostly, Dymphna had been guessing anyway. But in her clear imagination she had a picture of Dolores in the purple dress, a picture of handsome Baptist Geoffrey smoking, drinking, dancing under the palms in the Winter Garden and going – going where – somewhere the dress took her and she stood quite still while Geoffrey lifted it up-up-up over her head, brushing her fingers, tangling and catching in her hair, and then Geoffrey lifted her up and placed her on – on a bed, perhaps it was his bed and she was going to get into trouble back at the hostel because she was late-late-late. Like a late lament. And his kisses and caresses were so sweet and so chocolate dark and she was dizzy with desire.

Then, one day, Dolores borrowed the ten pounds from her sister and told her she had sold the coral necklace, and she said everything would be alright and she started singing 'cows are funny, cows are silly' and then, quite suddenly, her bottom lip unsmiling quivered and she began to sob. The next thing she arrives at the railway station, white as a sheet and comes home and goes into the bathroom and starts to bleed and bleed. And that is all. Father Gayle blessed her and forgave her sins, firm in the belief that she had made a final Act of Perfect Contrition. Dymphna prayed and prayed about that. Dolores was at least wearing her Miraculous Medal at the time of her death and so, chances are she went to heaven. Doctor Rush did nothing special. He signed the Certificate of Death. But Dymphna was holding the centre of a whole beaded shiny slippery spider web of lies, and could only keep saying she knew nothing at all. Rita did not believe her.

When Dymphna went to confession she confessed to telling lies, to withholding the truth. Father Gayle must surely have known the nature of some of the lies. The penance he gave her was an insult, so light and routine it did not touch her seething bubbling guilt – he gave her the Sorrowful Mysteries, and that was all. Dolores was buried in white.

Three years passed and one day poor weird Dymphna Marquand dressed herself up in a sequinned gown that had belonged to her long dead sister. She stood by the window as the afternoon sun came slanting through the glass, the rays hitting the sequins and throwing a strange pink cloud of liquid flickering light onto the white walls of the room. Then she ran, a glittering purple scarecrow down through the orchard and down to the river, the cocktail sequins of the mermaid marvel of the dress flittering and glittering and flapping. She must have tripped and fallen into the water.

The family and the police and the neighbours searched the district. Nobody found her for three full days. You could talk about madness and accidents and drowning – but not really about suicide. No, you could not speak of suicide.

After Dymphna died, it seems Rita never painted again. They buried Dymphna next to her sister in the churchyard, and twenty years later her sad father joined her, and only one year after that, her mother. Their older brothers were buried in bloodsoaked foreign soil.

So, as you can see, the picture of 'The Deedees' has a very special significance for me, as does the copy of 'Madonna of the Goldfinch'. I felt it was improper for me to ask Margaret and Jo-Jo if I could buy the goldfinch painting and so it still hangs, as far as I know, above the American bed in the old bedroom at 'Fatima'. A few months after my visit, I received from Margaret an envelope containing fresh copies of two small cracked black and white photographs. One was a picture of the Deedees playing under the blossoms in the orchard and the other was the Deedees again, with Rita. The girls are standing beside their mother who is seated at her easel. None of them is looking into the camera – Dolly is staring at the painting, Dymphna is staring at Dolly, and Rita is intent on her work, the paintbrush poised a few centimetres from the piece of plywood. She is painting 'The Deedees'.

HER VOICE

WAS FULL OF MONEY,

AND THEY WERE CARELESS PEOPLE

The Lisieux Convent. This was not situated as you might expect in rural France, but in Leafland, a 'comfortable, affluent' suburb of Melbourne, Australia. Such suburbs are often described as 'leafy', and this one certainly was lined with lovely European trees as well as rows of flowering gums all of which mysteriously did not suffer badly from the drought that gripped the country in 2007. Yes, the country was in the grip of drought. Rainbow lorikeets chattered, flittered and darted from the blossoms of the gums that bloomed forever in a kind of long long hot forever and ever. Summer, autumn, winter – the drought-affected gum trees sent out honeyed fluffy pink and creamy white puffs all across the leafy lanes. The aroma of the honey! Never had there been so many lorikeets living for so long among the flowers and insects of Leafland. They were luminously bright birds, all the colours of the rainbow in splashes and splats and stripes, if you looked at them up close. Some of the sisters at Lisieux were French, and the school was renowned for its success in teaching languages and music.

Olga Bongiorno was five when she went to school at Lisieux. She was educated there for the following twelve years – a dozen years from 1952 to 1964. She was from the beginning one of those girls whose broad linen collar was always starched white,

144

perfect as a seagull. In 1965 Olga went to the university, and then she went to the teachers' college, and then she returned to Lisieux where she taught French and English until she retired at the age of sixty. She herself would say if you asked her that she walked in the valley of the shadow and that she feared no evil. This grandiose biblical conversation-stopper concealed the death of a fiancé in a motorcycle accident when Olga was twenty-five. They never found the driver of the car. It wasn't as if Olga was a nun exactly, but it wasn't as if she wasn't one either, if you can follow that. She did one world trip with her sister and they went to London and Paris and Rome – and also Loreto where Olga was keen to visit the Holy House. She was interested in miracles. But Olga truly was happiest in her role as senior mistress of French and English at Lisieux, and she was mildly famous and widely celebrated among the families whose lives she touched through her years of teaching. As for what Olga did after retirement – those matters are not relevant to this story. For our purposes she is the Beloved Miss Bongiorno, sometimes known as Old Olga da Polga, named for the character of a guinea pig in a children's picture book. The guinea pig was a teller of tall tales, very tall tales, wild exaggerations. Nothing could be further from the character of Olga Bongiorno who resembled rather the aunt in a poem by Hilaire Belloc, an aunt 'who from her earliest youth had kept a strict regard for truth', Olga was a woman of high moral principles and a virtuous Catholic morality. What she saw and what she heard in and around her classroom were frequently matters of severe distress to her. She worried so about her girls, and was known to be, as a result of her anxieties, a devoted lighter of votive candles in the Chapel of the Little Flower.

Some of these things I tell you for the purposes only of clarification and ornamentation, since my focus is in fact on the year of the drought, the year 2007, and on Olga and her class of final year students of English. I should add at this point that Loyola, the brother school, was situated just three leafy lanes away as the tram runs. Now that Loyola has entered the picture, things are becoming more promising, and you can begin to sense where they are moving.

In Olga's English class in the year of the drought Marina Delaney was known to be sleeping with Caroline Herbert's boyfriend. The other girls in the group rallied behind and around Caro, and they turned on Marina in a pack. To the Loyola boy in the case (one Teddy Buchan) there attached, it appeared, no blame whatsoever for Marina's misdemeanours. Sometimes in the classroom it seemed to Olga that all eighteen cell phones vibrated and lit up in unison, as the news of the progress of the Marina-Teddy Affair travelled in thrilling bee-lines across the desks, down the leafy lanes, over tennis courts and football ovals, round and round the garden like a teddy bear.

Caroline wept. Marina wept. Juliette, Tiffany, Marie-Claire, Ching Ye and Veronica sighed and frowned and gurgled. Trinity and Pieta squirmed. Wanda the Giggler giggled. (Make a note of Veronica, and also one of Trinity.) It was not always possible, as you might appreciate, to teach the girls very much. Not that Olga had ever really understood, in all her years of teaching English and French, quite how the process of teaching really worked. Somehow her students ended up as literate, fluent, engaged, informed young women, but the chemistry or the physics or the metaphysics of the thing remained a mystery. All Olga knew at this point was that the Buchan boy was a terrible nuisance to her, that he was getting in the way of everything. He was the son of Buchan the leather-furnishing millionaire, and Olga knew his grandmother, Violet Fish, who had had her front teeth knocked out at the Lisieux vs Good Counsel hockey final in 1961. But that's really just another irrelevant little factoid. No, Olga couldn't get very much into the heads of her girls who were a flurry and sizzle of pink and grey dresses with the same huge white detachable collars as Olga used to wear. Some of theirs resembled hers in seagull snowy starch, but most did not. A little crumpled, a little un-white. Olga must proceed, and so the day arrived when the curriculum, like a tram on a track, brought them all to chapter one of *The Great Gatsby* by F. Scott Fitzgerald.

And still the bee-lines hummed in the zipped or unzipped side pockets of the pink and grey dresses. If you half closed your eyes those dresses resembled a shimmering, spreading splat of young and healthy brain tissue. Would Teddy ever go back to poor darling Caro? Would that slut Marina ever give him up? You can of course guess what happens here – on the tram Teddy Buchan meets the cute blonde mega-slut from New Hudson High, a tart in a short black skirt and tiny satin thong, and before you can say honey pot he's dropped Marina (serves her right), forgotten all about Caroline (brave but inconsolable) and has 'moved on'. Teddy, Caro, Marina, Mega-slut.

'Now girls, the plot turns on a hit-run accident.' The sleepy sun slants across the honey-coloured desks, stopping to glitter on the tiny diamond in the ear of Ginny King. Some phones glow and hum as the bee-lines are kept open. Marie-Claire has worked out the name of the evil New Hudson bitch.

'What, Patricia,' says Olga, 'is the correct procedure in the case of a driver who knocks down a pedestrian?'

All the pencils in Patricia's pencil case rattle across the timber top of the desk and sail down onto the carpet as Patricia suddenly sits up at the sound of her name. Her eyes are as blank as her mind. She doesn't know anything about the correct procedure.

'Anybody? Wanda?'

What is this procedure? I will tell you.

'You must stop, render assistance, call for help.'

This is news to the owners of the thirty-six eyes who are all on the brink of getting a licence to drive a motor vehicle.

'What? Why? Oh really?'

Myrtle Wilson was killed instantly, and the driver of the big yellow car, the death car, the car belonging to the Great Gatsby himself, put her foot down and drove swiftly on. To this information Olga's students register no surprise. So Daisy was driving the car and she killed Myrtle and left the scene at speed. So Myrtle had it coming. She was sleeping with Daisy's husband and she was only a slut anyhow. Daisy is Gatsby's girlfriend and long-time love, and she's as lovely as an ice-white blossom floating on a silver pool and her voice is full of money. She can disappear maybe into her money.

Wanda the Sleepy Giggler hears none of this. She is thought to be the richest girl in the school. Her father owns a city in the Middle East. Her mother is one of the Chicago van Cleefs. You might wonder what brings Wanda to Olga's classroom in the middle of leafy Leafland in the middle of the warmest summer since time began. Well, for one thing, her mother went to the Lisieux sister school in San Antonio, Texas, and for another it's a matter of the miracle of modern marketing. Leafland Lisieux has come a long long way in cyberspace since Olga was a child in a great white collar. Wanda will in any case be Finished at a school in Switzerland where there are princesses of all descriptions and of every stripe, and where her down-under bloom will carry an exotic cachet all its own. 'Drizabone Wanda Lust' they will call her, and they will wave a butter knife in her face gleefully crying 'This is a knife!' But that is all in the future and does not concern us here.

'They were careless people.' Olga tells them to write that down. 'They disappeared into their money.' Learn that quote. A few pens quietly scrawl the short quotations onto paper. A number of silent laptops register the words as well. It's rather nice, really, disappeared into their money. Pieta was editing her photos and had no time for quotations; Marina was composing an email to Teddy Buchan who was never going to reply.

Well, you can see how things were, and I am not exaggerating any of it. What would have happened if Olga had confiscated the phone? Anyway, she didn't. If anything I am being restrained and conservative and playing things down in the interests of fiction as against fact. But you can sense how this story is making its own bee-line towards a sharp and gleaming hot dry night in early summer when these girls have all closed their books and jettisoned their collars and have graduated from school with honours and accolades and laurel wreaths and stacks of valedictory books and higher school certificates and not a few glossy new cars. Pieta backed her lovely little Mazda into the muddy gurgle of the Merri Creek, and it is truly a miracle that she got out of it alive. Pieta is a survivor. Wanda is now on holiday in Florida with an aunt, so she is out of the picture.

So who, you wonder, is driving the death car in our story? Who is this speeding down steep Kennedy Hill Drive at three in the morning after a party to celebrate Teddy Buchan's eighteenth? It's Veronica Vale, deluxe dux of Lisieux, in her sleek green brand new Volkswagon. And who should come tottering barefoot and unbelievably intoxicated and wickedly wasted from behind a leafy elm where lives a watchful owl? Look, it's Trinity Maxwell in a glittering slivery silvery slithery slice of a wisp of Armani silk and sequin which she bought on e-bay. Through drooping yellow fringes of sunny yellow hair, with large grey eyes that almost focus, Trinity sees Veronica coming and she calls and waves, imagining in what you might describe as a split second that Veronica will stop and give her a lift back to Leafland. But Veronica is on the bee-line of her phone, talking to Caro who is passing out in Teddy Buchan's mother's ensuite and is about to get back in the pool with Teddy if he ever stops horsing around in the deep end with Charlie Beluga and a bottle of very expensive bourbon.

So a teenager is killed on Kennedy Hill at three minutes past three, and the dogs in the vicinity howl as the sirens worry and wail their way to the accident, the fatality, the tragedy, the waste.

Choose Your Own Conclusion
a) The driver put her foot down and disappeared into her money.
b) She stopped. She rendered assistance. She called for help. Yes, she called for help.

THE CHRISTMAS TREE PLANTATION

Everybody carries guilt for something. I tell this story in a feeble attempt to assuage my guilt for what I did long ago, when I was only fifteen, and I am now forty-four. It wasn't really a big thing then, but it took on a terrible dimension in my heart, later. I can never say sorry, never be forgiven. Can I forgive myself?

I need to tell you first the story of Gary McGill, a recluse living on the outskirts of Finton, a small town in central Victoria.

Six months ago. Gary died alone in his shack on the other side of the pine plantation. They were cutting down the trees for Christmas when somebody wandered into the shack and found the body. It turns out he shot himself. He also shot his dog Misty. The place was full of rusty old junk and rabbit skins – and hundreds of Gary's little paintings. He used to walk into town every so often to get supplies of oil paint, as well as cigarettes and vodka and packets of rolled oats. I suppose he was on a disabled pension. He built a wall of empty vodka bottles. He more or less lived on rolled oats, and used to cut up the boxes to use as canvases. So you've got all these pictures of the landscape around here, on bits of cardboard. He'd prepare the surface with thin glue, just as though he was using canvas, and then he'd get to work. He could do just about any style – Boyd, Drysdale, Smart, Monet, Turner, Cezanne, Matisse, Picasso, Rousseau

– you name it. The weird thing is there's nearly always a tiny little figure of a young woman just visible, just present in the scene. The repetition is creepy, I have to say. And these pictures were just lying around the place more or less like litter, all curling slightly, not quite flat. And Gary and Misty lying dead on the iron bed, decomposed and chewed by animals. Definitely suicide, the police report said. No question.

It's pretty sad. Gary came from a wealthy farming family in Finton, went to art school, kind of lost his way, and by the time I knew anything about him, he was the strange hermit in the shack on the other side of the plantation. When I was going to high school, I remember seeing him only a couple of times, in town to get his supplies. He would have been about thirty. I was fifteen, and I thought he was exotic and handsome, but quite scary. He was always filthy. I left Finton and went to the city to go to art school myself, and since then I have worked in galleries in San Francisco and London, where I live now. I still think of Finton as really being home, and I sometimes go back for Christmas.

A lot has changed, but the McGills are still there in their mansion on the hill, and these days they also have vast racing stables. It's the fashion. The funeral was private of course, but the story of Gary's suicide stirred up the whole town and surrounding area. He apparently didn't leave a note. Just the piles of curling paintings. I wonder what the family will do with them. Everybody wants to own one now. It's kind of disgusting I think, like vultures. However, as it happens, I do own one.

I've always been fascinated by it, for several reasons, as you will see. In fact it now hangs in the hallway of my place in Camden Town. It has great sentimental value for me. But much more than that. I framed it – so it's flat at least. If anything it resembles a Rousseau crossed with a Magritte. Dense dark pine trees with the lighted window of a cottage glowing coldly through the gloom. And just discernable in the doorway of the cottage is the solid little figure of a girl in red.

So how did I come by the painting?

Well one of my friends in high school was Moira-May French, and it belonged to her. She said she met Gary in the newsagent's when he was buying paints, and she asked if she could see his pictures, and he gave her one to keep. I now think this might have been a lie, but I believed her then. Actually, I don't know how she could stand the smell of him. For some reason that now escapes me, I pinched the picture out of her schoolbag and never got the chance to give it back. For a joke, I told myself. Some joke.

Now this is another sad and mysterious story. One Christmas Eve when she was only sixteen, Moira-May disappeared and has never been seen since. Christmas Eve. It's funny the way things will sometimes focus on one time, one place, almost as if there really is a pattern. Maybe there is.

I was away at the beach with my family for the holidays, and we read in the paper that Moira-May was missing. She ran away on Christmas Eve in the middle of a big family row. She was a teenage runaway, and she has never been found. The police finally got the story, such as it was, out of her parents. She had told them she was pregnant, and she wouldn't name the father, and she ran out of the house and disappeared. Forever. Is anything forever?

I suppose it's possible you have put two and two together by now.

When they eventually demolished the shack they found Moira-May's pregnant little skeleton buried under the floor. Her schoolbag, full of Gary's brushes and paints, was even hanging on a hook above her grave. Anybody could have found it, long ago, if they had been looking.

I am haunted by images of her running up the hill through the pines, running in desperation to the arms of her strange lover, her dark hair flying out behind her, her eyes bright with terrible tears. She tells him she has left home, she imagines she will stay with him, that he will protect her and the baby.

He shoots her through the heart.

I need to get back to London. I need to take down the painting and study it. Forgive me, Moira-May, for stealing it from you then. Forgive me. The picture is your memorial. The tiny image of the girl in the doorway speaks to me of my guilt.

LIFE SAVING

WAITING FOR THE GREEN MAN

One broad leathery purplish leaf was bent over at the tip. It resembled, in some ways, the head of a cobra. Striped veins, forest green, crept deeply through the purple. On the soft point of the leaf hung and hovered and quivered a fresh droplet of water. Faith Starr watched with silent concentration as sunlight hit the drop, as sudden splashes of sparkle blazed on the end of the leaf.

It was early afternoon. The year was 2009. The place was a suburb of an Australian coastal city. The garden of a church rectory.

The tall row of cannas grew all along the fence in a wilder part of the garden. During the very hot summer the scarlet floppy flags of their blooms had blazed high on stalks above the leaves. Faith, wife of Christopher Starr, Rector of St Michael and All Angels, had planted the cannas long ago. The rectory garden was Faith's responsibility. She had planted the blue spruces — one of these had become the parish Christmas tree, decorated every year with coloured lights, branches sheltering the crib that Christopher had bought in Assisi once upon a time. St Michael's was one of those 'high church' parishes where they have incense and a great deal of old-fashioned ceremony. Faith had a fondness for it and its traditions and its people. Old established families with names that echoed the brass plates along the interior walls of the church. Young couples with babies who, in spite of the dignity of the ceremonies, were welcome to crawl along under the pews, pushing little cars and rolling teddy bears. Strange homeless people in tattered clothing. Tourists too, coming to experience the dignity of the worship, the glory of the music.

This afternoon in autumn Faith was reclining on the cane garden lounge, resting before going to town to buy provisions. The bishop was coming to dine. He would stay the night.

The expectation was that the bishop was about to deliver the news it was time for the Starrs to move on. They were in their early fifties, and there was work to be done in the regional parishes in the country to the far north of the city. Out in the bush, in the outback, far away in the wilderness where life could be hard, the climate harsh, the people parched, in need of relief, rain, and spiritual guidance. The Starrs had no children so were not encumbered by family responsibilities. It was time for a change, in the mind of the church, perhaps even in the hearts of the Starrs.

Faith was in fact fond of the bishop, always looked forward to his arrival, although this particular visit carried a freight of fear and apprehension. The unknown is after all the unknown, and the familiar is safe. Safe enough. She would miss the people of St Michael's, miss her garden. What about Martha? Would they be able to take Martha who helped with the house and was known to them as 'the Efficacious'? This had been home for so long now, and the people of the parish had become Faith's family. It sounds very like a cliché, but this was exactly as it was.

She planned to drive into town to visit Ted her favourite butcher and get a free-range chicken to roast for the bishop's dinner. There would be one of her wonderful salads followed by her celebrated strawberry shortcake and homemade ice-cream. The wines were Christopher's responsibility. He kept a wonderful cellar. Martha the Efficacious had already set the table, elaborate with white damask and heavy silver, candlesticks, and a wide Wedgwood bowl of full blown roses, glowing pink and yellow and red and mauve. Once again there is much to describe as cliché in the lives of the Starrs, and once again, that was the way it was, a cosy, old-fashioned, stereotypical life of the rector, the wife, the servant. Some might call it stuffy, stultifying, quaint, even something from another planet, and certainly from another time.

Thoughts of all these images and matters floated through Faith's mind as she lay on the cane lounge and contemplated the drop of glittering water that hung on the cobra's head. She would close her eyes for a few minutes, then she would squint. The rainbow in the droplet was momentarily released to her vision.

In spite of all her busy Wedgwood and roses and candlesticks, her pleasant reclining on the cane lounge, the rainbow shimmering on the water drop, the sweet devotion of Martha, something was missing.

The empty heart at the heart of the full life at the rectory was the absence of the child. There was only ever one child in question. Early in the marriage their baby daughter was born but she was already dead. Faith appeared to put the experience behind her and get on with her life, their lives, the life of the parish, the devotion to the church, devotion to the garden. Martha forever there, in the background, in the foreground, supporting, initiating, being. Faith was celebrated for her generosity and kindness to others, for her ability to organise the fête and the jumble sale and the study groups and the youth groups and the coffee mornings and the choir and the garden party and the cleaning of the brasses. 'The angel par excellence of St Michael and All Angels' the bishop often called her, favouring the company with his deep episcopal laugh.

Far from forgetting the baby, Faith frequently let thoughts of her float across her consciousness. Zoë was the child's name. Zoë Alice Starr. They never spoke of Zoë. Lost, gone, she never was. Curiously, Zoë was not listed in the prayers for the dead that were spoken at St Michael and All Angels every Sunday. After a period of deeply private mourning Faith picked up the pieces (as her mother said) and sailed on with life. The baby inhabited her thoughts, but gradually Faith gave no outward sign of this fact. The baby's ashes, contained in an antique carved ivory sphere from China, were buried in the garden, beneath a rambling rose. Félicité et Perpétue bloomed in pale pink bunches that dangled from the branches, petals falling onto the earth where Zoë lay. Faith tended the rose bush quietly and diligently. She tended every rose in the garden, lovingly, quietly, diligently. That was the way Faith was. She would dead-head the roses and Martha would call her in for lunch. A small chicken sandwich and a cup of coffee in a thin white cup.

One day, a long ten years after the death of the baby, Faith woke up in the morning aware that she had, as Christopher might have said, 'lost her faith'. It had just gone. It must have been diminishing all that time, and suddenly it had gone. Ping! None of the things she thought she had believed made any sense to her any more. Not the Gospels, not the angels and the saints, not Easter, not Christmas. Not prayer. No sense, no sense at all. She had not had a dream, not had a revelation. Nothing special had happened in her life that she could think of. It just seemed that one day she could say: 'I believe in one God' and so on and so forth, and mean it, and the next day the words had no significance for her at all. A strange sweet emptiness came to occupy the place where belief had been. The resurrection of the body and the life everlasting. What on earth could that mean? Somehow, there seemed to be no point in discussing this with anyone, particularly not with Christopher. To do so would be to unpick everything, to abandon everything, to let slip the established routine of life. And without the established routine, where would she be? It never even occurred to her to discuss it with Martha, and she had no special friend. No sister. Faith was alone with her unfaith, with her garden, with the earth of her baby's grave, and the knowledge that down there among the roots of Félicité et Perpétue lay the Chinese ivory ball.

So the garden parties and the study groups and the services and everything went on just as before. Faith (and the irony of her name did not escape her) took part also in all the church services just as she had always done. Singing the hymns and saying the prayers and taking Holy Communion. She did not even think she was a hypocrite. It was somehow as if she were desensitised to her own thoughts and feelings and behaviour. She was moving through her own life in a strange trance. Was she suffering from depression? Was she going mad? She did not ask herself these questions. She went to funerals where everyone professed to be 'in sure and certain hope' of the life to come. Saying Grace at meals. Wearing the gold cross Christopher gave her when they were courting. Lighting the votive lamp before the little statue of Mary bought long ago in Austria. Opening the ladies' meetings with a prayer. Smiling. Laughing. Praying. Being.

Occasionally it occurred to her to wonder about the meaning of good and evil. She wondered about the soul of Zoë Alice.

But if she didn't believe in anything any more, what meaning did the baby's soul have? Félicité et Perpétue grew more and more dense and blossomed like a cloud in summer. Sometimes Faith thought that perhaps her faith might return, that this place where she now found herself was in fact the dark night of the soul. She still read and loved the poetry of St John of the Cross. She might come through, come out of her dark night, be strengthened, illuminated. But she was not worried, went blithely on as the wife of the rector Christopher.

She cast her gaze on such lovely things as the sunlight on the drop of water on the tip of leaf, she inhaled the primrose perfume of Zoë's rose, and she knew that she was observing and participating in the good. This knowledge gave her a soft melody of pleasure. She appeared to live her own life in a gesture of grace.

'Faith takes such joy in simple things,' Christopher would say to people, speaking with fondness and approval.

Faith sometimes felt that she moved through life as if in a fairy tale, feet just above the ground, obeying magical rules, following a story that framed her and sustained her. Where once she had prayed in the private silence of her mind and heart, formal prayers, informal prayers, requests, acknowledgements, now she found herself expressing wishes and desires. And these, the wishes and desires and prayers, all seemed to be really much the same in effect. Some wishes came true, as some prayers had been answered.

A psychologist might say that the failure of God to answer the prayers for the life of Zoë Alice would be the key to the decay of the religious belief. That could be true, but Faith did not think of it. All she thought was that one day she was a believer, and the next day she was not. And yes, of course, her faith just *might* come back. But really, she was not concerned. God, or whatever it might be, moves in a mysterious way. One oddity in all this was that she could not stop herself from whispering quite often the prayer to St Michael. 'Holy Michael Archangel,' she would say, 'Defend us in the day of battle…' Although she did not have any sense that a day of battle was imminent. The words were a lovely incantation. Perhaps she was moving to a place where words had no real meaning, or had a different or a higher meaning than she had thought.

Well, the bishop was coming, and she needed to shop for dinner.

She drove to town and parked the car and took her two calico shopping bags to the Italian fruit shop for the strawberries and greens, and to Ted the butcher for the chicken. On her way back to the car she came to a busy city intersection, waited for the lights to change, one calico bag in each hand. She had just missed the green light. These lights would flash red and amber and green. Images of little red men striding out and little green men striding out appeared in the middle of the lights. Faith always imagined herself as waiting for the green man, a man, not a light or a signal, but a man. She liked the green man. When he appeared, the music of his step – ticky-ticky-ticky – would tell the people to brave the dangers of the road.

As she waited, still as a statue, a little singing in her brain went:

'Holy Michael Archangel, defend us in the day of battle. Be our safeguard against the wickedness and snares of the Devil. May God rebuke him, we humbly pray, and do thou, Prince of the Heavenly Host, cast down to Hell Satan and all wicked spirits who wander through the world for the ruin of souls.'

She stood at the kerb, wearing her stylish lemon linen coat from the jumble sale, her sensible black shoes planted neatly on the kerb, her body hemmed in by a pack of pedestrians. A great phalanx, trucks and buses as well as cars, was held in check, just, by the red lights on her right and on her left.

The last stragglers were crossing on the amber warning light straight ahead. The traffic was champing at the bit on either side of her. Leaping lions and sabre tooth tigers vroom vroom ready to pounce and surge. Holy Michael Archangel, defend us in the day of battle. And just as the lights did change, releasing those beasts from their captivity, just as the red man non-walked into view, there in the middle of the intersection was a scurrying young mother, baby on her hip, mobile phone to her ear.

Time was warped into one of those split seconds you some-times hear of. The scurrying figure on the road almost tripped. The baby almost fell. The phone clattered to the ground and separated like a broken insect into two black shiny parts.

And in that split second a powerful lemon yellow figure, its arms outstretched in majesty, appeared before the traffic that was leaping forward on the right. With one huge magnif-icent gesture, the angel arrested the flow. Stopped the traffic like a great celestial policeman. For the split second the traf-fic stopped, the yellow angel glowed unearthly. Its wings were vast and quivering with beauty and power. On the end of each muscular angelic arm whirled a soft white calico pouch filled with heavenly magic. The woman with the baby scooped up the black particles of phone, clutched her baby tighter to her hip, scuttled headlong across the road and dissolved into the crowd. The angel itself flew back before the traffic came, withering into a shadow among the dark grey bunch of the pedestrians. Dissolving into air.

Faith Starr stood where the angel might have been.

When the green man came on with his jaunty walking legs, ticky-ticky-ticky, the people all moved forward in safety, and time moved on. Faith Starr crossed the road with the crowd, got in her car and drove home. She worked with Martha in the kitchen, and together they produced a magnificent meal.

The bishop said the blessing in Latin and the Starrs both murmured their amens. The finest strawberry shortcake on earth was served. Over the coffee and brandy with nougat and dark chocolate leaves the bishop delivered the anticipated bombshell which was accepted with grace and aplomb and resignation. Time to move on, new pastures, the challenge, the need, the dedication, the call. The large and varied parish. The career. The ambition. The vocation. One day, Christopher will be a bishop himself. Imagine. Bishop Starr in all his glory and regalia. Bishop Starr's wife, in a silk coat and lovely hat.

In the kitchen Martha the Efficacious watched the news. People were claiming to have seen an angel in the city. A woman with a baby said an angel saved her baby's life when she dropped her mobile in the path of the oncoming traffic. Martha brought this amazing little titbit of news to the table when she carried in the second pot of coffee. It lightened the mood which had acquired an overlay of awkwardness as the company contemplated the upheaval of moving the Starrs to their new and enormous parish.

'Perhaps it was St Michael himself. I am quite sure,' pontificated the bishop, smiling broadly at Martha's story, 'that there are angels aplenty, Christopher, in the regions. You will see, Faith, there will be ministering angels doing more than stopping traffic out there in the bush. I imagine they probably take a hand in the cooking and the garden.' He laughed his round episcopal laugh. 'But first I expect they might help with the packing. There may be some things to leave behind? Much to take with you. Much to take. Even your beloved roses, Faith. You might take cuttings. The new rectory needs a garden. It's a bit of a wilderness, I am afraid.' He beamed.

For another split second, Faith thought she somehow understood that the bishop could see into her heart and mind – she couldn't say her soul, for she didn't believe she had a soul. Then she suddenly thought the bishop didn't really believe in her soul or in St Michael and the angels any more than she did. She realised that somehow they were, all of them, participating in a lovely elaborate game. Even Christopher? Yes, even Christopher. Surely not! All except Martha, who probably *did* believe. Things shone when Martha touched them, and Martha brought a kind of warmth with her presence. A deep peace, was it? She had already said she was willing to move to the new parish, and Christopher and Faith were both grateful for that. So, it must be said, was the bishop.

When the rectory was dark and quiet, when the bishop was snoring in the guest room, when Martha was sleeping sweetly in the small bedroom off the pantry, when Christopher's eyes were closed, his breathing steady, Faith put on her robe and slippers and went into the garden. She saw the tall dark shadows of the cannas in the moonlight, the beloved outline of the spruce. She breathed in the perfume of the tobacco plants and the roses. She came to the pale cascade of Félicité et Perpétue.

The ivory ball of ashes was not deep below the dewy surface of the earth. With a garden trowel Faith, kneeling, turned the soil, and soon she scraped the hard intricate surface of the ivory. She lifted it from its resting place and cradled it in her hands. It was ingrained with dirt, but it shone. Her tears hovered, quivered then trickled from the corners of her eyes. She brushed the ivory ball with her fingers, held it to her lips, and she carried it with her into the house.

She would carry it with her wherever she went. She would carry it with her.

Into the wilderness.

HE PAINTED CUPIDS ON SOUP PLATES

All lines of longitude converge at the Poles. The South Pole is at 90 degrees South latitude. The island of Tasmania lies at 42 degrees South latitude and at 147 degrees East longitude. All things considered, this is not an ideal location for the smallish heart-shaped piece of land (known as Tasmania, after the Dutch explorer who discovered it in 1642, the year the English Civil War began, the year Isaac Newton was born, the year Galileo died). It would have done well to have been islanded a few degrees further north, perhaps somewhere around 30 degrees where it could bask in sunshine and perhaps grow breadfruit, who knows? These days, now that the twenty-first century is here, with the rise of sea level and the rise of temperatures, it probably doesn't need to move after all. But there it was in 1955, drifting in the chill of the Southern Ocean, and that is where the story of the man who painted cupids on soup plates has its centre, close by a town called Deloraine (named for Sir William Deloraine, a character in 'The Lay of the Last Minstrel' by Sir Walter Scott), on the banks of the Meander River (possibly named after the Meander in County Mayo).

The girls arrived at Melrose Abbey in Deloraine by car and coach in early February. They came driving along the avenue of silver poplars leading up to the front porch, a stately procession.

The year was long ago in 1955 and the weather was really quite warm for this part of the world. The Misses McInnes, one round and fat and jolly, one tall and thin and possibly dour, were there to greet the girls, standing as statues beneath the portico of the Georgian house built long ago, so long ago, by labourers who came to the remote spot on the Meander in the service of Josiah McInnes, free settler, dairy farmer, husband of Moira, father of many sons and daughters. The history of the house, a Tasmanian landmark, was printed in the prospectus for Melrose Abbey Finishing School, a document devised by the jolly one, Veronica, with grammatical corrections by the possibly dour one, Harriet. By a little quirk of fate, Veronica was inclined to pessimism, whereas Harriet was an optimist, thus subverting their stereotypes.

And so the girls arrived, in 1955, to be finished by the Misses McInnes. Wendy Archer, Jennifer Dabner, Myra Mandeville, Robyn Woodhouse, Yvette Bowen, Jacqueline Marsden, Sonya Jones, Princess Aldegonda of Naples. There was always a member of minor European royalty or aristocracy among the group, giving this school a cachet almost unknown to such places on the mainland of Australia. Harriet had a contact in London who was able to supply her with these desirable exotics. The other students were all Australian or Tasmanian, about sixteen years old, had survived the Second World War and the epidemics of polio and tuberculosis, and emerged more or less gleaming and healthy from their homes and schools to be polished and finished in the lovely fresh air behind the little town of Deloraine on the Meander, in the shadow (so to speak) of the rounded blue peaks of the Great Western Tiers.

They came here to be far from the troubles of the world, to be separated from the distraction of young men, to be prepared for Life, principally in all its highways and byways of the commerce of matrimony. Conversation and Skiing and Fishing and Gymnastics and Literature and French and Art (History, Theory and Practice) and Music (History, Theory and Practice) and Philosophy and Grooming and Deportment and Speech and Dance and Needlework and Cookery and Hospitality and Woodwork and Flower Arranging and Book-keeping and Typing plus Shorthand were promised. Such a wealth of knowledge and information parceled up there at 42 degrees South, 147 degrees East. Students were free to choose their subjects, the only rule being that in the end they must graduate in at least eight different fields. You can see that it would be possible to achieve in, say, Conversation, Skiing, Fishing, Grooming, Deportment, Speech, Dance, Art and leave Melrose with a Certificate of High Excellence and no knowledge of French.

Apart from the Misses McInnes and their brother Keith who taught Art, and the French wife of a Polish sculptor, the staff consisted of four female McInnes cousins who were variously trained in a broad range of subjects and who came in from the town of Deloraine most days. One of these cousins, Judith, had been to business training college in Melbourne, and managed the Royal Oak Hotel with her husband. She taught the Book-keeping and Typing and Shorthand. Another one, Belinda, taught the Cookery and Needlework, and also supplied the tartan wool dresses and heavy navy blue cloaks which were the principal uniform of Melrose Abbey. Nobody, with the exception of Veronica who had spent a year at a mainland college for kindergarten teachers, had any background as a teacher, but their dedication to their students was unmistakable. Various girls from the town drifted in and out doing the cooking and the cleaning and systematically pilfering small items of clothing and jewellery. The garden and odd jobs were done by two old brothers called Jim and Jake who were more or less interchangeable.

There had been some student failures, as is only natural. (Famously, a girl called Sunshine Feathers from Lower Snug in the south of the island had absconded with the barman from the Westbury Inn and they had ended up in Alice Springs from where her father went to reclaim her, only to have a heart attack and die. Sunshine never came home. She and the barman went to Lightning Ridge and were never really heard of again.) Girls came for two years and often left to travel to Europe for further broadening and buffing and polishing. (Who could need more? people wondered.) At the end of the two years another group would arrive to be greeted by the Misses McInnes. Melrose Abbey had a high reputation for its choir, regularly taking out first prize in the eisteddfods which were celebrated in several towns throughout the island. Once the girls had been taken by boat to the famous mainland Royal South Street Eisteddfod in chilly Ballarat, where they had again triumphed in their dark tartan dresses with huge white collars and emerald green pussy bows.

Above the lintel, over the heads of the Misses McInnes as they stand there waiting to greet the group, carved into the golden stone are the words:

'The way was long, the wind was cold,

The Minstrel was infirm and old', the first lines of 'The Lay of the Last Minstrel'.

And so they arrived, on that February morning, Wendy, Jennifer, Myra, Robyn, Yvette, Jacqueline, Sonya, Aldegonda. Aldegonda was accompanied by her own companion-chaperone, a young Swiss woman named Sofia who paid, it seemed, little attention to her charge, spending much of her time walking and attending to her own diet and general appearance. Chopped fruits and seeds, fresh air and exercise. She was perhaps handsome but not pretty, and spoke many languages. She was of a fidgety dispostion, and always wore a fresh flower pinned to her blouse, and shiny neat brown pointed boots on her tiny feet. She and Aldegonda chattered to each other in Italian, but Sofia could switch back and forth with great facility into English or French. Her English resembled that of British royalty. Her French – who knows?

The girls themselves were fresh faced and hopeful, bearing large suitcases and cabin trunks and tuck-boxes of fruit cake and sweet biscuits to sustain them through who knew what days and nights of finishing. Aldegonda's tuck-box contained only slabs of nougat wrapped in rice paper and seven bottles of a rather inferior brandy which was placed in the wine cellar to be brought out on Sunday afternoons and shared. Sofia seemed to have an endless supply of her seeds and grains and also dried fruits which she took with her to the breakfast table. She was evangelistic about this, and willing to share, although the only person interested was Yvette who was allergic to eggs. Myra, who was the class comedian said eating Sofia's breakfast food was like eating birds' nests. Sunday was a day of indulgence. There was no religious content whatsoever at Melrose Abbey, the name of the place being purely literary, nostalgic, and fantastical.

I could beat about the bush here, take you skiing and fishing and making patchwork quilts as a way of building suspense and red herrings, but I might as well tell you first up that brother Keith and companion Sofia caught each other's eye. That is the something that happened in 1955 and it was most exciting for all concerned. Just like the girls, you were searching around among the boys from town and Jim and Jake and Keith for the promise of romance. Well, it was Keith. I have described Sofia, but I should also describe brother Keith.

Keith McInnes, youngest child of the family, was born in 1930, and in 1938 he contracted infantile paralysis (or poliomyelitis). He survived the disease but his wasted limbs meant he would be crippled for the rest of his life. He was expert with his crutches, in the manner of story writer Alan Marshall. His skill with a paintbrush was legendary in the district, and his portraits, pictures of houses, and local landscapes graced many a wall and mantelpiece. He also did miniatures in oval silver frames, and decorated china. He was not really handsome, but he had a dazzling smile and a soft, perhaps seductive laugh. Those pilfering girls with their dusters and brooms were a little afraid of him, saying that his dark eyes could see right into your soul. They avoided him.

But the dark eyes lit upon companion Sofia, and Sofia's heart softened. She began to take part in the painting classes alongside Aldegonda (who had quickly become known as Allie). The girls are always on the alert for any whiff of romance, and naturally they are aware of the chemistry between Sofia and Keith. He paints a little plate for Sofia, a plate with cupids on it. Allie alone denies the romance, maintaining that Sofia is simply being polite, and saying the others could not be expected to understand European manners. It is curious how the minder and the minded have changed places, with Sofia at risk and Allie in charge. Well, truth to tell Allie is jealous. That's the thing here, the Neopolitan Princess feels she is losing Sofia who is her possession. She could not care less about Keith, no, she does not want him for herself, she wants, owns, Sofia's attention, and she has lost it to Keith.

Did Allie splash Sofia's hand with boiling butter in the Cookery class? I think she did. Did Allie mix sawdust from Woodwork into Sofia's breakfast cereal? She certainly did. Did Allie nick Sofia's edelweiss pendant and throw it down the well? Yes. And one of the town girls took the blame, whatsmore. Did Allie realise that her childish carry-on was counter-productive? No, she didn't.

But came the day they all went fly fishing with Harriet on the Meander. Willows drape the river's edge. It is a golden afternoon. Harriet is like a rugged Scottish highlander with her canvas knapsack and her brilliant home-crafted flies. She has even succeeded, perhaps by virtue of her own passionate interest, in teaching the girls to fish. They are quiet and attentive. She catches a small trout. Wendy, who displays real talent, catches a large one. Myra gets her line snagged in a willow branch.

Sofia and Keith are sitting alone at a bend of the river, beneath a weeping willow, beside an old stone bridge, beside also the swiftly running waters of the Meander. Out of sight, out of earshot.

Perhaps Allie had planned what happened next, perhaps she acted on impulse. She had left the others behind and crept along under the bridge to spy on Sofia and Keith.

Suddenly she threw herself fully clothed into the freezing water. Help! Oh Help! She called, and at the moment she meant it. What did she expect to happen? Did the stupid girl know how deep the water was? It was deep. Would Sofia jump in after her? Would Keith throw her a lifeline? What lifeline? Oh Harriet, Harriet, come quickly, quickly. But Harriet and the others are in fact far away; they do not hear the cries. Sofia ran towards the bridge, and in confusion stood stiffly on the edge as Aldegonda of Naples struggled in a panic in the river, her woollen skirt and jumper gradually taking on the water. She held on to a low overhanging tree branch, but it was very slippery and she would soon have to let go. Keith moved swiftly along the bank on his crutches until he was as close as he could get. He balanced on one crutch, leant over, extended the other crutch to the girl in the water.

And then it happened, Keith toppled into the water, Sofia could not even scream. Aldegonda hooked her elbow over the branch, and, as Keith was swept past her, she crawled along until she was free of the river. She fell onto the bank. It was then that Sofia began to scream. And scream.

The inquest into the drowning of Keith McInnes concluded that his death was accidental. He was awarded a posthumous medal for bravery, having sacrificed his life in the attempt to save Aldegonda. Sofia and Aldegonda were collected by two sombre Italian men who arrived late one night and instructed them to pack their bags at once. Nobody was standing on ceremony. In great grief and sorrow the Misses McInnes closed the school, and all the girls, with such a tale to tell, scattered to the safety of their homes.

The way was long, the wind was cold.

Curiously, Myra seemed to be the most affected by the tragedy. She sought consolation in a convent in France and in due course rose to be the mother superior. Sofia returned to Switzerland where she eventually married a prosperous inn-keeper. When Aldegonda's horrified parents gathered their little daughter to their breasts, they asked her what had happened. She told them she had fallen into the river and the brave painter had saved her, but he had drowned. She explained that he did lovely china paintings, and she had in her luggage a little souvenir he had given her. It was a soup bowl decorated with pink ribbons and blue hearts and flying cupids. 'It will always remind me of him,' she said. 'He was very well known for these soup plates with the cupids. It is very Tasmanian, very typical.'

GOING TO ST IVES

As I was going to St Ives,
I met a man with seven wives,
Each wife had seven sacks,
Each sack had seven cats,
Each cat had seven kits:
Kits, cats, sacks, and wives,
How many were going to St Ives?

Our street was affectionately known as 'The Hill'. On an electric light pole at the bottom of it there was a sign saying: 'This is a War Savings Street', a sign that stayed put long, long after the war was over. I mean the Second World War. The houses on The Hill were full of pre-war, war, and post-war children. I was a war child. Lawrence Vale Road ran along the base of The Hill, and Punch Bowl Road was within walking distance. These are their real names, and they are so delicious to me that I am unable to change them in order to conceal the location of this story, which was Launceston, Tasmania. The names of the people, however, I will change. You can call me Nalda. Nalda the war baby. Then there will be Caroline Rivers and Loretta Lilley the post-wars. After I had invented their names I searched those names on the internet and of course there were real (I suppose) people who were dentists, artists, fashion designers bearing those names. I intend no reference to these people. I suppose it is almost impossible to invent a name.

As far as I knew, the children who lived on The Hill had been conceived in a normal way and born in a local hospital. I was born in a converted Edwardian mansion called St Ives. Pause for the nursery rhyme – As I was going to St Ives, I met a man with seven wives. The house had been named for St Ives in Cornwall, a town that owes its title to a holy Irish maiden, Ia, who sailed across the sea on a leaf, landing in Cornwall, bringing the Christian message in the fifth or sixth century. You have to admit that is a *lovely* story. My head was full of such stories, and my life was also nourished and illustrated with the details of the real lives of the people who crossed my path. That sounds a bit sinister – 'crossed my path' – as if I was lurking in the shadows, predatory, fox-faced. But I think it's accurate. And I tend to think that life sometimes, quite often in fact, operates like a fairy tale (or a myth or one of those things). And remember I once went as an unborn child to St Ives – crossed the path of seven wives – each wife had seven sacks – each cat had seven kittens – kittens, cats, sacks, wives, how many were going to St Ives?

In Punch Bowl Road there lived Loretta, and in Lawrence Vale Road lived Caroline, and they, post-wars, were both adopted. I was only six when they arrived on the scene, and I am surprised now to realise that my mother told me about the adoptions. I was not supposed to spread the word, and there is something in my nature that loves to hug a secret close, so I didn't tell. But the knowledge certainly coloured my relationship with Caroline and Loretta.

Caroline from Lawrence Vale Road was the adopted daughter of my mother's friend Elvie Rivers, and Loretta of Punch Bowl Road was ditto of mother's friend Bonnie Lilley. Elvie and Bonnie were quite unlike each other, the common threads here being that they were both friends of my mother, and that they both adopted baby girls at the same time.

Here's a snapshot from my memory of Elvie. She was tall and slim and proper and not very pretty. Her house had a clipped box hedge (Mr Rivers was a loyal and dignified husband who worked in an office at the woollen mill, and kept the garden shipshape) and a path of crazy paving that led between flower borders and lawns to the front steps which were made from green concrete. Immaculate – that's the word that comes to mind. Elvie's place was immaculate. If you caught her unawares in the morning, she would be wearing a floral or an embroidered apron, and would have her hair up in a net. In fact she resembled a housekeeper who might have been employed to spic and span every surface in the establishment, and woe betide a spider that thought to spin a web up in the corner of a room. No mouse had ever dared cross her threshold. In the afternoons she sallied forth in dress and coat and hat and gloves and handbag, with wicker basket. Believe me when I say that Elvie's basket had a bunch of gumnuts painted in autumn shades attached to the side. In her house, on a pink bedspread in the guest bedroom Elvie had her china doll, an Edwardian creation of utter perfection and terrible fragility. I had occasionally been invited to gaze in wonder at this treasure. Not to touch. She was just called 'The Doll'. Elvie was my mother's friend from childhood, and had a reputation for being naïve and gullible. My mother and her sister used to pretend that chocolates came out of the taps in their house, performing sleight of hand amid muffled laughter. Did Elvie really believe them? I don't know. They said she did.

Now for Bonnie. She was short and fat and round with tiny hands, feet, teeth. She wheezed when she laughed, and was generally more common than Elvie, but of course hat and coat and gloves went on when she went out. She too was a childhood friend, but canny, one who would *never* fall for the chocolates trick. She was a great knitter, as was my mother, and they were cooks too – cakes and scones and so forth, and they were smockers. Elvie was not skilled in any of these things. I think her gift was dusting and polishing. Mr Lilley was a problematic figure, some kind of worker who came home in greasy overalls, was silent, and I thought menacing.

Loretta Lilley slept in a most amazing contraption. It was a large wood, metal and wire cot painted pale green. Shaped like a house, it resembled a huge hutch for a lucky rabbit. I found it shocking and terrifying, and the memory of it makes me feel ill. Did it come from an orphanage, the cot? Did the visiting nurse think it was a good thing? Caroline Rivers had no such cage. More a crown princess than a lucky rabbit, she occupied a pink and white nursery where the cradle was a hanging white wicker basket, and the cot was a romantic white dowling affair custom-made by a local carpenter who happened to be my uncle. The coverlet was a concoction of lace and frills and ribbons. Everything around Caroline was white, with touches of pale pink, while everything around Loretta was brighter, more casual, even multi-coloured. Loretta wore a bonnet knitted by her mother in a riot of rainbow bobbles. I admired this bonnet, was truly impressed and attracted, although I made the mistake of comparing it in conversation to a tea-cosy.

Incidentally, The Doll was put away, spirited somewhere, and as far as I know Caroline never saw it. I asked her about it when she was about ten and I was sixteen, and she said she didn't know. I now imagine that The Doll had served its purpose, and that Caroline herself had taken its place.

The men who had (I presume – but I could be wrong) no agency in the manufacture of the baby girls seemed to remain outside a field constructed by the woman and the child. It did not seem to me that they existed and played a part, in the way, for instance, that my father and the other fathers on The Hill played their parts.

Anyway, the Rivers and Lilley marriages were infertile, and both couples wished for a child. Once upon a time there lived an old woman and an old man…etc. I am not actually suggesting they were old. Yes, well it seems that after the war there were babies aplenty to choose from. Caroline and Loretta were chosen. They were the lucky ones. The Rivers and the Lilley households were also lucky. Perhaps there were people linked to, but now outside the story who were not so lucky, not so happy. Of course there were.

From time to time Elvie and Bonnie would wheel Loretta and Caroline up The Hill in identical cream wicker prams to visit my mother. When the babies had been admired, and the women were settling in for afternoon tea and a good gossip and exchange of secrets, the prams, with netting fly covers were parked outside under the apple tree. I was posted out there and instructed to report any cries or other irregularities. 'Nal is very good with babies.' And I was. If they were awake I entertained them with a green felt mouse, tickling them and making them laugh. My mother had told me (in confidence, remember) that these babies were very lucky, and that their families were blessed, and that the presence of Caroline and Loretta in the neighbourhood (War Savings Street) and even under our apple tree was something in the nature of a miracle.

The war was still very much on people's minds in the mid-forties. There was some sense in which these children were the promise that wars were over now, that life under the apple tree was going to be different. I should point out that this particular apple tree was next to the underground air-raid shelter that had become a playroom, lined with pastel coloured maps of the world, and still furnished with tin cups, and gas masks, and canvas stretchers on which to sleep. There were rugs and pillows and printed instructions about things to do in the event of enemy invasion.

All went well. I used to give my old hockey sticks and tennis racquets to Loretta. Caroline always got shiny new ones. Loretta had a natural musical ability and was an *incredibly* diligent student at school. Caroline was a compulsive liar and truant, her mother (naïve, and gullible) believing everything she said. You could argue the nature/nurture question over and over, but I am not sure you would get anywhere. Who were these children, really? Does it matter? I do know that Loretta grew up to be a highly responsible and productive adult, and that Caroline grew up to be the opposite of that. Where they are now, I don't know.

They never became friends with each other, so different they were hostile. But there was a dramatic summers day when their paths crossed. These girls who had so early in their lives crossed my path, are about to intersect with each other.

They are fifteen, both of them sunbathing and swimming with different groups of friends in the pool that was on the lawn at a place called the First Basin of the South Esk river. It is Caroline who decides to swim not in the pool but in the river, along the edge of which are signs warning of danger. The waters are deep, frothing and eddying over ragged rocks, flowing down towards the Cataract Gorge. I probably don't need to tell you, as you will have guessed already – but Caroline nearly drowns and Loretta dives in and saves her.

I used to tickle them with the green felt mouse in their prams under the apple tree, beside the entrance to the back yard bomb shelter. Their photos are in the paper: 'Lawrence Vale Girl Saved From Drowning.' Lucky rabbit saves crown princess.

'So look at this,' I say to my mother. 'Loretta has saved Caroline's life.'

And she says, 'Well fancy that. Good Heavens. What happened?'

'Caroline was swimming in the river at the Basin, and nearly drowned. Loretta saved her.'

'That's fate, you know,' she says. 'Those two were destined. You may not realise it, but they were both adopted. At the same time. From St Ives. At *exactly* the same time.'

'You told me that – that they were adopted. When I was six and I used to play with them under the tree.'

'Did I? Why would I do that I wonder? It was a secret. They were supposed to be non-identical twins you see. War babies. Well, post-war babies really.'

'Impossible.'

'More than likely.'

'Hearsay.'

'Gospel truth.'

Wise nodding of the head. Clicking of the knitting needles.

'They ought to get their records.'

'They can't. It was a private arrangement. Money changed hands. No documents.'

'Not even at St Ives?'

'Specially not at St Ives.'

'What does that mean?'

'Oh Nally, it was all a private arrangement, like I said. It was all so long ago. What does it matter? Life's a riddle.'

'You mean the Lilleys and the Rivers *bought* the babies?'

'I didn't say that.'

End of conversation. Life was a riddle.

And as for the other riddle – How many were going to St Ives?

There are two answers, depending on whether the man and his wives and so forth were going to St Ives or not. Sacks don't count because they are not living creatures. So the answer is either 'one' being the teller of the tale, or 2752 plus one – for the teller of the tale. But in my own case you would have to add two – that's me and my mother, making it 2754. And then there's St Ia on her lovely little leaf-boat. I think you have to add her. Mind you, the legend goes that she was met in Cornwall by seven hundred and seventy-seven companions.

And so the tally mounts.

ESSAY

THE STORY OF THE STORIES

'I will wear him in my heart's core, ay, in my heart of heart.'
HAMLET

I grew up in Tasmania, and in my mind, in my heart of heart, the island's shape resembles that of a love-heart. When I hold in my hand a chocolate love-heart wrapped in scarlet foil, I may think, for a fleeting moment, of home. The idea of Tasmania often appears in my fiction, and it flitters throughout the stories in this collection. The map of Tasmania is often left off the map of Australia. Not only is it inconvenient to put it in, a little island afterthought at the base of the continent, but it is also an easy scapegoat in Australian jokes. Its physical beauty, wild land-scapes and fine produce are matters of envy for the rest of the country – people like to visit the island as tourists – but it also lends itself to contempt and derision. Some of its history is dark and ugly, a history of which the people have been traditionally ashamed. Today I believe it lags behind the other Australian states in economics, education, literacy, and I don't know what else. When I was a child I felt that the place where I lived existed, if it existed at all, in a special kind of nowhere. I thought this was exciting, actually. And I began, when I was about fifteen, to collect odd little references to Tasmania in the literature of other places. I now have many of these. As people used to say 'Timbuktu' to mean faraway and romantic and un-serious, they also used to – and still do, in fact – drop in the word 'Tasmania' to mean faraway and insignificant, and yes, romantic. Even fantastic. I recently heard that there is a language called 'Tasmanian English' but I don't know what it is.

Australians sometimes see Tasmania's shape as that of a woman's pubic hair, or as a little piece of excrement from the anus of Australia itself which is seen as a big bum. Or the island, according to islanders, is a lone testicle dangling there, fertilising the continent. I return stubbornly, sentimentally, to the image of the love-heart.

So you see, the 'Tasmania' you will find moving in and out of my stories, although not apparently or necessarily conforming to anything I have just said, is freighted for me with a great deal of meaning. I am always on the alert for new and old information, forever musing, at some level, on the realities and unrealities of the place – where I no longer live. Consider King's Holly (*Lomatia tasmanica*). This is a plant that is more than 43,000 years old. It grows in the wilderness of south-east Tasmania, and when I say it is 'a plant', I mean that there is only one example of it in the wild. While a single plant can live for 300 years, it is sterile and reproduces only by cloning from bits of itself. So you see, it is most precious. Startlingly endangered. I suppose I keep my memories of, notions of, and tenderness for Tasmania lightly alive for myself in my fiction. It nestles in my heart of heart. And if a collection of stories is anything, it's the writer's heart of heart.

The writer is telling stories to the reader, and these stories can take different forms. They might be written in the first person and the present tense, for example, but this is not to say the action is taking place at the time in which the reader is reading. And it is also not to say that the first person is the writer. Behind the voice of every story is, of course, the mind and hand of the writer.

The writer is making all the choices, deciding on not just the sequence of events and the characters, but on the manner in which these elements will best be delivered to the reader. The writer chooses the language. The writer chooses the tone. One of the writer's most important tasks is that of inviting the reader into the story, assisting the reader to participate in the mood and therefore the meaning. But – a big but, this – the writer is not in fact the storyteller, for the storyteller is located in the voice of the narrative. Fay Weldon is one of my favourite writers, and everything she writes is delightfully coming from Fay Weldon, but the storyteller is not Fay Weldon, writer. The storyteller is the narrative voice. And perhaps I could refer here to one of the epigraphs to this collection: 'We make fiction because we *are* fiction.' This short statement unsettles and to a degree subverts the common discussion about the differences between 'fiction' and 'non-fiction'. It highlights the mystery that exists at the core of writing, for writing *is* a mysterious process. I hope to illuminate parts of the mystery, only parts of course, in this essay.

A reader will find throughout this collection, and in fact in the fabric of much of my work, a reference to and flavour of old fairy tales, in particular the tales of Grimm and Andersen. The motifs and plots of fairy tales, repeated over centuries, changed and yet paradoxically immutable, can have a powerful grip on the human imagination, informing and shaping thought and feeling, which in turn have an effect on the stories themselves. Movies have for many years mined the plots, characters, images and motifs of the fairy tale which seems to be a bottomless trove of fascination. Human society seeks happiness and perfection, and tales are a medium via which these states can be promised. Yet behind the tales lurk the obvious truths of the everyday world, rendering the stories ever more seductive.

The words 'happy ending' or 'happy ever after' can usually raise a simple smile of hope, or at least a wry smile of the hope of hope. A small child recently said to me: 'Cinderella will die in the end, you know.' She realised the sad truth, and yet she is still prepared to be led into hoping or believing otherwise. Although the ending of 'From Paradise to Wonderland' seems to be happy and resolved, there is a clear threat of imperfection in the final comment. That's the thing about stories, isn't it — they come to an end. But there is a sense in which each story is only an episode in a vast narrative.

I have been captivated by tales since I was a child, and I realise that my own writing has partly grown out of that interest. I was given a collection of Grimm's tales when I was six. It had a dark blue cover embossed with gold, and the illustrations were monstrous little black etchings by Cruikshank. I read 'The Juniper Tree' in amazed horror, and my imagination returns frequently not only to the tale, but to the feeling it aroused in me. There is a strange purity to fairy tales, a quality of being removed from reality, of operating by special rules, and yet there is also a quality of being able to enunciate the facts, the truths of the everyday in terms that are universally comprehensible, that chime deep down with the beats of the human heart.

Sometimes when I think about writing I imagine a divide between what is called memoir and what is called fiction. Yet I also realise that both forms often resolve in the telling of a 'tale'. You can begin *any* narrative with 'once upon a time' and get the job done. The element of a promise of fantasy widens the territory that the writer can explore for the reader. I return to the lovely words of Russell Hoban: 'We make fiction because we *are* fiction.' That is a statement of a truth that might go deeper than anybody wants to go.

<u>MY HEARTS ARE YOUR HEARTS</u>

'My Hearts Are Your Hearts' is set in Adelaide, at the Writers' Festival. So it's a story for writers and readers, about writers and readers. The incident with the chocolate hearts is something I observed at a festival. Writers were sitting behind piles of their books, greeting fans and signing copies. The matter of the love-hearts was a small ill-mannered gesture, of little consequence really. But it tickled my imagination somehow, and led to the telling of the story – a common enough story at any sort of conference – of sex and transgression. And I loved the idea of putting the two writers together – the woman from Tasmania who writes popular romance, and the man from England who writes successful 'literary' fiction. The ending simply made itself, giving me great delight in the writing. It's a little light meditation on men and women, popular and literary fiction, and how the game might be played.

It's told from the point of view of an omniscient narrator, in a kind of plain tone of voice that is one of my favourites. It's a bit flat, a bit matter of fact. This voice gives me, the writer, the chance to reveal the politics of the story through the words and behaviour of the characters without intruding, yet guiding the reader about where to look and how to listen. You will find this voice in many of my stories. I suppose this one is a story about several types of human folly.

When I had chosen this story as the one that would provide the title for the collection, I realised I had written another one about a real heart, a transplanted organ, and this led me to place next to them the story about the transplant of the uterus. So I could group them under the heading 'Body Parts'.

'Diane's Fiancé's Ex-Wife's Brother's Heart' tells a story from the nineteen sixties, when heart transplants were new and utterly amazing. 'Back to the Womb' tells a twenty-first century story of the transfer of a uterus in 2014 from one body to another. In 1967, when Dr Christiaan Barnard moved Denise Darvell's heart into the chest of Louis Washkansky, the whole world was amazed and agog. Organ donation is now more routine and almost un-remarkable, such that the first successful transplant of a uterus in Turkey in 2011 attracted less attention than the heart transplant of 1967. Then in 2014 Swedish doctors successfully transplanted nine wombs from nine living donors into nine other bodies. I saw a TV documentary about it. The nine women reminded me of the nine ladies dancing in 'The Twelve Days of Christmas', and even of the twelve dancing princesses in the fairy tale. Little old songs and nursery rhymes sometimes drift into my prose. These things are distant melodies that play with and against the issues raised by the narratives. This time they didn't make it into the story, but they almost did.

News of the Swedish case was of course reported world-wide, but I suppose nothing is ever going to equal the splash made by Christiaan Barnard in the sixties. The account of the womb transplant can come as a shock to a reader, right after the lighter tale of the chocolate love-hearts. Readers don't necessarily read the pieces in a collection in the order in which they appear, but in putting these twenty stories together, I offer one trajectory, one logic – there could have been others. I could, for instance, have put the heart transplant story second and the womb story third, giving them their historical sequence. Or all the body part stories could have come last in the book. Or they could have been scattered throughout. And so forth. I give you a reading order, but you can choose. For that matter, I could have placed this essay first, but I suppose that might de-fuse some of the reading of the stories.

It wasn't until I read the first three stories over in sequence that I saw how they play off each other in ways I had not recognised. The details in the heart transplant one in particular seem to me now to offer metaphoric confirmation for the events in the womb one. Well, that's a way of looking at it.

BACK TO THE WOMB

The point of view and the tone of voice are so very important in any piece of fiction. I find that these elements of the telling usually come to me with the story itself, with the material, with the characters. 'Back to the Womb' was inspired by the TV report – one young woman received the uterus of her own mother in 2014. The relationship between the two women inter-ested me, and suddenly the narrative tone was there – kind of casually conversational and mostly without names or places. To begin with the narrator invites the readers in, invites the readers to imagine they are a young woman without a uterus.

In everything I read about uterine transplants were the words 'large chunks of blood vessels'. These large chunks had to be taken from the living donor. Each time I read it, in the middle of sober medical writing, I was shocked by the 'chunks'. Such a cold, vulgar, brutal noun. Could they have said, for instance, 'sections'? Were the doctors so nervous for the survival of the donor that they couldn't help saying 'chunks'? It was this word that gave me the warning for the tragic outcome of my story.

Stories tend to take on a life of their own, and I found that 'Back to the Womb' had a specially vigorous life. You often hear fiction writers say that characters appeared suddenly out of nowhere – and I think readers might find this fanciful talk. However it does happen, and I can tell you that Auntie Primrose, known for most of the story as 'Auntie P', shouldered her own way into this narrative, and worked a kind of magic on the plot – which had threatened to be too terribly tragic. Primrose, representing a generation that grew up before the advent of organ transplants, somehow earned the right to the use of her name, whereas the modern characters are all just represented by letters. Believe me when I tell you that I had no conscious control over this fact. They came with their Ys and O&Gs and ITs; Primrose came with her fancy name. But then it all comes full circle when the baby – who is the real point of this whole complicated saga – gets Primrose's name which invests the future with a deep bright optimism.

It is funny to be analysing my own story in this way. All these things are there, and I put them there, but I didn't do it in any deliberate way. As an analyst of the story, I am almost as fresh as any other reader. Perhaps the key question to ask is where did the story originate? Well I suppose it was brewing away ever since I first heard of transplants – that would have been 1967. Then in 2014, I saw the documentary about the uterus transplants in Sweden, and the story leapt into life, into ordinary Australian suburban life. Quite a long gestation.

DIANE'S FIANCE'S EX-WIFE'S BROTHER'S HEART

'Diane's Fiancé's Ex-wife's Brother's Heart', set in an upstairs flat near the Royal Melbourne Hospital, was inspired by the TV images of Fiona Coote, the sweet young woman who received the first Australian heart transplant in 1984. These days it is possible to know the origin of donated organs, but I think I am right in saying that back in 1984 the donor was anonymous. So the characters, with their own reasonably complicated lives, are free to speculate about the origin of the heart that was given to the pretty girl who advertises milk on television. There is plenty of anger, mixed with trivia, in the hearts of the characters, their anger underlined by the behaviour of the menacing woman down the hall. One character has searched her own memory and imagination for the possible origin of the girl's new heart. Into her own hum-drum daily existence she can now bring the tragedy and drama of one man's death, and can re-ignite her feelings about that death by obsessing about the girl in the milk ad. The girl's life must have been filled with drama and tragedy too, but to the people in the flat, watching her on the screen, she is – well, she's not really real is she? This begins to get into the familiar overlap between TV and day to day life, but the story doesn't concern itself with that, other than to see the girl's image as the focus of interest, emotion, and the location of the heart of the dead man – who is in fact quite distant from the characters in the story, as signalled by the complicated title. These characters are living in the middle of the noise from the traffic on the road and in the sky, constantly aware of the drama and tragedy associated with ambulances and helicopters. They are living with the delusions of the woman down the hall. They are living with the nonsense of department stores and Father Christmases. It's a story about damage really – the damaged people everywhere – the girl with the heart being, for the moment, a winner in the contest of everyday life. The story is in the first person, from the point of view of the young woman who thinks she knows where the heart came from. So the tone is not at all ironic, but it has an urgency – she's just telling a friend about how life is, and it isn't really very pretty.

The chocolate hearts of 'My Hearts Are Your Hearts' are in fact a long way from the heart that beats in the girl in the milk advertisement, but in my imagination the chocolate hearts and the real hearts chime unpleasantly across the narratives. What you are looking at, as a reader, when you open a collection of one writer's short fiction, is the working of that writer's imagination, at how the writer's response to experience is shaped into stories. Sometimes the stories in a collection will follow one theme or one subject – you could have a collection all about organ transplants – but this book isn't one of those. I have, in hindsight, perhaps for readers' pleasure, grouped the stories under headings, but these are fairly general. Readers frequently ask writers where their ideas come from. In my comments in this essay I attempt to put forward some evidence of where my stories might originate – as much for my own interest as for yours. Something reviewers like to do, in their search for a way to describe a collection, is to point to the fact that the collection doesn't follow a particular theme or subject, and is therefore inferior. This always puzzles me. Some do, some don't, so what? And I have to say that now that I have assembled this collection, and have re-read the stories in order, with this essay in mind, I actually find that the collection presents, in all its divers ways, a particular angle of vision, a take, if you like, on life. Mine. I didn't really know it would do that, but I suppose it's no real surprise. I am so used to reading comments about how collections don't live up to reviewers' expectations of some sort of cohesion, that I was not prepared. Here you have my sensibility, my moral perspective. If you take issue with those, that's OK. The binding agent here is the exploration of the nature of the human heart.

<u>FROM PARADISE TO WONDERLAND</u>
There isn't just the question of where the ideas come from, there's also the question of why write a particular story at a

particular time. Quite often, it's because one has been asked for a new story for an anthology or some other publication. The first story in the second section, 'The Laws of Love', was written in response to an invitation to contribute to the *Review of Australian Fiction*. It's a love story. Also the story of a murder. I decided to include the story 'From Paradise to Wonderland' in my book on writing *Dear Writer Revisited*, and to write a detailed description of how the story came into being. In the explanation I say that the 'mechanism of the story started to tick away like a little clock'. That's quite a fair account of how stories can develop. Here are the points I highlighted.

One The origin of the house that is a key element. I live in the country, and was on the train to the city. This was when my writing mechanism was in the process of getting a story to send to the *Review of Australian Fiction*. The journey is familiar to me, and I always look out at one point along the way to gaze up across a vineyard to an impressive sprawling house on the top of a hill. People say that two brothers built this house, and lived in two parts of it with their families. The families, so goes the myth, quarrelled, and the house had to be sold.

Two A small point that also came from the journey is the matter of how Anka's mother was supposedly smuggled out of Poland. The train stopped at a suburban station, and on the platform there was a billboard. It was an advertisement for a newspaper. The picture on the billboard was a huge photograph of Mirka Mora who is a beloved Australian artist. She was described on the billboard in type as a grandmother; she looked sweet and charming, and was holding a pretty china teacup. I know Mirka, and I can imagine the fun she must have had constructing that image. In the type alongside was information about Mirka, including the fact that she was a survivor of the Holocaust of World War Two. I took a photo of the billboard on my phone. The woman in the seat opposite me saw me do this, and she said: 'Oh, I had an email about that woman just this morning. She used to smuggle babies out of Germany in her handbag. In the war. She was nominated for the Nobel Prize, but Al Gore got it.' Oh, the wonders of storytelling.

I love this woman on the train for her easy ability to bounce in and out of fact and fiction and fantasy. I didn't invent her, by the way. Well, she invented herself I suppose.

Three Suddenly the house on the hill and the war in Europe came up against each other and the mechanism of the story started to tick away. By the time I had been to the city and had boarded another train and got home that afternoon, I was ready to start writing.

Four The voice of the narrator Tabitha spoke the first sentence, and the story was up and running. Now where does a writer get that narrator? That is one of the mysteries – sorry about that – of the process. She, the character, the narrator, leapt up, leapt out, and there she was, telling the story of the house. She was talking in 2013, and the story begins today, goes back twenty-three years so she can tell her story, and returns to 2013 at the end.

Five Structure – I didn't know where it was going to end. All I knew was that she used to live in the house, left the house, and was telling the story. It was one of those cases where the storyteller within the fiction seems to take over from the author of the whole thing. As I have suggested before, you hear writers say this happens – some writers say it never happens. Some say it shouldn't happen. I just revel in the fact that it does happen. I don't write out plots – I just let the story take me along with it. There is a beautiful drive and energy. But it is my world, my history, my newspaper cuttings, my fellow travellers that find their way into the fabric of the story. And I am not suggesting there is anything wrong with writing out plots, either.

Six In the period following World War Two Australia welcomed people from countries such as Italy and Poland, and they brought with them customs and traditions that have become part of life in Australia. The vineyard suggested Italians to me, and so the brothers were Italian. Then I got into the idea of the mixture – the first generation of Anglo-Australians to marry the Europeans. And then there was the Polish girl. So the subject matter began to foreground the issue of migration and social change. I wouldn't say I set out to write a story about those things.

Seven I have a friend who says she wishes life resembled the world of Beatrix Potter, and I think she is not alone in that. People often lean towards a comforting fairy tale and long to inhabit it. To their peril I think – unreality can take you too far from reality. The Beatrix Potter world got into the story with Tabitha's name, a name that places the narrator in a particular stratum of an Anglo-Australian ethos.

Eight As I was writing the story, I was also working as a contributing editor to the *Griffith Review* for their November 2013 issue, the topic of which was the fairy tale. So fairy tales were on my mind. The first fairy tale element that made its way into the story was the use of the name 'Gretel'. I didn't think about it – it just appeared. I left it there. It is always possible for a writer to change anything in the work later, but Gretel seemed right, a German name that played neatly with the suggestion of European migration. I had no idea at the time of Gretel's arrival in the narrative that she was in fact a key player. The word 'Wonderland' also came of its own accord, and obviously took the story where it had to go.

Nine Also at the same time as the writing of the story, the government of New Zealand passed legislation legalising same sex marriage. On the TV news I saw a placard in the crowd outside the court. It showed the image of the Disney Cinderella kissing the Disney Snow White. Those two famous profiles suddenly coming together lips to lips. And so there were Gretel and Tabitha in each other's arms at the end of the story. It turned out to be quite a journey for Tabitha. The movement from 'Paradise' to 'Wonderland' gave the story its shape and its structure.

Ten It is always important to get the time frame right. Although there are no dates given in the story, the narrative is anchored in the war and migration details, and so I set out a timeline for myself, making sure the ages of all the characters – from the mother who named Tabitha, to the career of her granddaughter Skye as a dancer in New York – were logical.

Eleven The central drama of the story is the murder of one brother by the other. That is the event on which the story turns. Always human nature and human relationships. Reality seems to have killed off Tabitha's poor mother, by the way. Well, it was all shocking, wasn't it.

Twelve I have said little about the actual writing of the story – the sentences, the paragraphs, the vocabulary, the rhythm. Those things come with practice. And if there is one thing a good piece of writing has it's rhythm in the prose. It's always a good idea to read your work aloud so that you can listen to the beat.

Thirteen And they lived happily ever after. Or did they? The story isn't going to tell you.

I think that's enough points.

Writers often say they don't know what they are writing about, really, until they have finished. And one doesn't usually indulge in the flurry of analysis I have outlined here.

It has occurred to me that one of the attractions the short story has for me both as a reader and a writer is the ability the form has to provide moments of illumination, to draw together delicate strands of emotion, character, incident, theme, subject – and to do something akin to what a conjurer does with coloured silk handkerchiefs, pulling them all in to make a ball, and then, with a flourish, opening them up as a brilliant full-blown rose. The stories in this collection are really intended to please and to entertain the reader.

This Wonderland story is also in the first person, but this speaker, unlike the one in the heart transplant story, is actually giving the narrative of her own life with its joys and sorrows. It has the warm tone of one to one, of someone taking a listener through the key points that have brought her to the happy ending in Wonderland. Again I find it hard to explain how a story ends up having the tone it does – but it seems to me that every narrative presents and unravels with its own imperatives of various kinds, as if those characters and those events require that way of telling. It can be a nice exercise for a writer to tell the story several times from different angles, different points of view, in different voices, tones, tenses. I did that in an old story of mine called 'Woodpecker Point', and the process was very enjoyable.

HIGHWAY TO HEAVEN

'From Paradise to Wonderland' is one of the stories in which Tasmania is a key element. The next one, 'Highway to Heaven', is set far away, in Spain and in America. *New Australian Stories* asked me for a story, and I can't explain why I thought of writing 'Highway to Heaven' – for some reason I remembered meeting a Spanish priest who later ran off to South America with a woman who came to his house selling toothpaste. That little fact had always delighted me, and it came forward as the germ of the story. But of course a writer has to assemble a lot of other detail in order to make such a treasure into a narrative. You sometimes hear the advice: 'write about what you know', and sometimes you hear: 'write about what you don't know'. I think both ideas are a bit nonsensical in their strictness. You really always do both, don't you? I have always been interested in teeth, hence in toothpaste – although I have never heard of a person selling toothpaste door to door before or since. So that was what I loved about Lauren to start with. She was going to come out on top. And from the detail of the toothpaste which was the turning point in the lives of Lauren and Josu, grew the broad web of the highways of the USA, the business of art – with the little insect of Annette marking her place in the story – and the dark mysterious background of the Church.

The death of a character can set off a chain of events, and I started this story with the death of Josu, building up, in a third person past tense narrative, his life before and after meeting Lauren. The structure presented itself, as it were, around the fatal meeting with Lauren. Without the disappearance of Annette, maybe Josu wouldn't have run off with Lauren. Annette was the forerunner. I know I often say I did something in a story 'for some reason' – and of course those reasons are largely what writing fiction is all about. They usually remain inscrutable. They're the elements fiction writers freely, sometimes unconsciously, recognise and use – if that isn't too utilitarian a way of looking at it all. Or too mysterious.

MY BELOVED IS MINE AND I AM HIS

I wrote 'My Beloved is Mine and I am His' in response to a news story about the Anglican Church. So this was not a tiny scrap of inspiration, as is sometimes the case with my stories – this was a whole big narrative. I no longer remember what was in the news and what I invented, but I don't think that matters. My story exists for itself. It tells of cruelty and transgression, and the breaking of vows, and the breaking of the laws of love. There's a terrible foreshadowing of what's to come in the embroidery Patricia, the main character, does as a child. I wonder how I thought that up? It's the 1950s this time, in rural Australia, just before the 'sexual revolution', and the narrative moves kind of relentlessly from go to whoa, taking different points of view from time to time, different voices, offering flashbacks too. Even stream of consciousness – what an old-fashioned term that is. Sometimes it is told in the past tense, sometimes in the present. The story itself demanded this of the writing. As I say this, the story sounds complicated – it isn't – it required those devices, but they fall naturally in with the narrative itself, with the characters, with the history. The tone of this story is completely soft and un-ironic, creating an atmosphere of strange and quiet horror. The ending of the story grew out of the tragic, damaged character of Patricia. I think it shocked the character, Moira; it might shock you; it shocked me.

MONKEY BUSINESS

'Monkey Business' is in the ironic conversational tone of voice I often like to use when writing about life today. Children's parties are big business in this affluent rapacious all-consuming society that is Australia. I heard of one party where there was a performing monkey. It set off the story, which speculates about the future of the planet, locating the heartbreak of this in the broken lives of a five-year-old girl and the monkey at her party. It's also about the relationship between daily life and the internet, and about marriage breakdown and its collateral damage. I do believe that fiction is a powerful way to address the big questions – I hope that through the story of Charlie I have dramatised how I feel about endangered animals, the endangered planet, endangered love.

PERHAPS THAT BIRD WAS WISE

When the mother of a friend was dying, the friend used to read to her from a big book of old fairy tales. That's the inspiration for 'Perhaps that Bird was Wise'. The inspirational nugget is a tiny thing, in a way, slipping into the narrative quietly. Tasmania gets a mention. My interest in the fairy tale shows up here. It's really a rather everyday story of family life, its ups and downs, its little satisfactions and sadnesses. And another inspiration was a line from T.S. Eliot that kept coming back to me. The one about 'too much reality' being hard to bear – the woman in the story, although she lives very much in the real world with all its difficulties, has an ability to find satisfaction and solace in fantasy. She wants to live, not in the world of Beatrix Potter, but in the house of the three bears, as depicted in certain illustrations.

One thing I do in this story – I address the reader on the subject of the plot. I say that the reader and I both know what fate is going to do, although the character doesn't know. This is consistent with the tone of the narrative which is a bit bouncy and skippy and conversational. It's about love and romance and destiny – and death hovers over it, as death will.

WHERE THE HONEY MEETS THE AIR

Australian Love Stories requested a new love story, and the one I wrote was 'Where the Honey Meets the Air'. I do enjoy responding to a defined task, and I think – well I know – that the stimulus and the limitation of an invitation can be marvellous for the writing of short fiction. The narrator of this story is a man who lives a very privileged existence in the bosom of his wife's family. It's set in the Melbourne suburb of Brighton, and in prosperous rural Kyneton. How does a writer make those decisions about a story, when the story is all made up anyway. Well, I suppose it has to be set somewhere, and this man seemed to fit right in to Brighton and Kyneton somehow. Maybe I just saw the name of the town on the board as the train drew in and out, and so placed the family there in rural splendour and safety – or so the narrator thinks. The character is like a child really, running away from difficulty into the haven of home. Journeys – walks, trains, trams, aircraft – are useful to a fiction writer. The imagination seems to be stimulated when the writer is in the process of going somewhere.

The tone of the honey story is particularly conversational, chatty, as the narrator searches for words and ideas to express the terrible story of a love triangle. He keeps trying not to tell the story, but the listener can feel it pushing forward all the time until at last it becomes clear. He has a keen interest in words and narrative, being a playwright, and he keeps commenting on these aspects of what he is telling. There's a funny kind of innocence about him – this just developed as he talked to me. There I go, saying a character talks to me, makes himself up. That's how it sometimes happens.

Those were the stories I grouped under 'The Laws of Love'. So many different meanings, so much joy and pain.

One of the main topics of fiction is death, and so here are stories under the heading 'Sudden Death'.

WAITING TO BE SEATED

I wrote 'Waiting to be Seated' in response to 9/11. I thought of giving it the title 'Catch Me if I Fall'. I think I was in two minds about the title because I was very nervous about the story, about responding to 9/11. I read a short magazine article about a woman who left a lovely green dress in her hotel room in New York. It was ruined by the ash in the air. I realise I love green dresses, always have, and what triggered my imagination here was the green dress in the magazine. This gave me my inspiration for the story. Loss, of course, is the real topic. Green is, if you are superstitious, an unlucky colour. The happy, hopeful life stories of Maggie and Dom from Ashburton build up behind the terrible ending.

<u>HARE</u>

The Great Unknown is an anthology of supernatural stories edited by Angela Meyer. I was invited by Angela to contribute, and so I wrote 'Hare'. I hardly ever write supernatural things – this was fun. Fortunately, at the time of the invitation, a friend told me that she had been twice out walking in the bush recently, and had encountered a rabbit that stopped and seemed to want to talk to her. A long time ago another friend told me about a cat that stopped in her path and really did talk to her. I have such friends. Usually these stories, while fascinating, don't inspire me to write fiction. However this time, the time of the rabbit, the anecdotes seemed to be a gift to (or from) the Great Unknown. I thought a hare was more mythic than a rabbit, and did some reading about the mythology of hares. Something I love to see is a field of sunflowers – although since the downing of MH17 such scenes have taken on a chilling sinister feel. Writers for *The Great Unknown* were asked to remember the TV show *The Twilight Zone* as possible inspiration – weird creepy stuff that mostly remains unexplained because it's inexplicable, and there-fore hovers in the imagination in a horrible way, half real, half un-real. Elements of real life come up against terrible mysteri-ous dark forces, and people get caught in the middle. So I just blamed the hare for everything, but left it mysterious. The photo on the postcard at the end of the story tells you as much as there is to tell. It's nice the way Poirot unravels the plot for you at the end of an Agatha Christie – *The Twilight Zone* doesn't unravel – the logic is quite different. It's the Great Unknown. I imag-ined an eerie soundtrack to my story as I wrote it, and images of the characters and scenes presented themselves to me with great visual clarity. The hare was particularly scary. From my reading – not all of it mythological – I learned about the hare's kinetic skull, like the skull of a snake. But that didn't get into the story. I think this is the only story I have written in which a character writes a confession – the structure demanded it.

ON THE MOUNTAINS OF THE MOON

'On the Mountains of the Moon' is another Tasmanian story. It's about truth and the internet and malice, and the way the events and feelings of the distant past can come back to haunt you. The inspiration came from a friend who made the common mistake of googling himself and finding that ten years before somebody had posted his death, complete with accurate details of his life and family. He doesn't know who did it, and just laughs and brushes it aside, but I reckon it was somebody who hates him, for some reason, from way back. The narrator has the wondering tone of a reasonable woman, but she also has the wit to see that the internet post has its roots in the games, emotions and events of childhood, and of who knows what about whom.

NO THROUGH ROAD

'No Through Road' was inspired by a story I heard a long time ago about a woman from Melbourne who ran away from her husband and bought a fabulously expensive – or so I thought – raincoat in Paris. Well of course there always has to be more to it than buying a raincoat, so I provided the rest of the narrative, telling it in the third person with a few little asides from the narrator. I wanted to highlight the inter-connections between people at a certain level of society. The raincoat, plus alcohol, is ultimately responsible for sudden death far off in Cambridge. As you can see I like to pull out threads and weave them across the story, giving them their moment in an unexpected way.

<u>THINK OF ME</u>

Attics and cellars and garden sheds are the storage places, resting places of sorted and unsorted memorabilia. In an old suitcase in one of these places I re-discovered a tiny tin box on the lid of which were printed the words: 'Think of Me'. Inside was an old photograph, given to me by a friend, of a small girl. This picture in the box set off the story 'Think of Me'. In the suitcase there were other photographs, a random pile of images I have loved and collected. One in particular stirred my imagination. The girl is standing in an open doorway in some unknown European city. Above her, a half-circle fanlight ornamented with iron curlicues and two iron swans. Before her a short flight of worn stone steps. Behind, the darkness of the interior. On the tall wooden door are scratched some words I do not understand – and also a diamond shape that somehow resolves itself in the outline of a heart. As if almost in the middle of a little dance step, the girl holds her hand across her heart, and her face is sorrowful. Another version of the picture, where the girl has turned to face the camera, is on the cover of this collection, by kind permission of the photographer Griff Clemens – who told me the city was Dubrovnik. The story I wrote is another Tasmanian one, perhaps because distant memory is often located there for me, and the girl in the doorway, on the threshold, has a haunting quality. She is poised between the future and the past.

The narration of 'Think of Me' is very plain and sad. The journeys of two people, one going to Hobart in the expectation of great happiness, the other in grief. Coincidence operates in this story, and it can be an awkward element to deal with in fiction. Here it is key to the plot, but it is muted, and, I hope, convincing. Such coincidences do occur in 'real life' but a fiction writer usually tries to avoid them. The details of the story came to me on a flight to Hobart, but almost everything about them is invented. One source of inspiration was a display in the airport of remarkable photographic postcards by a local photographer who had recently died.

THE LEGACY OF RITA MARQUAND

'The Legacy of Rita Marquand' is set in Tasmania. When it was first published someone wrote to me asking some questions, under the impression that it was a memoir. It's pure fiction, but I can understand the mistake readers do make with a first person narrative. The inspiration for the story was the purple sequinned dress. I still have the original in my possession. It came from my mother's early life, moved through the dress-up boxes of my childhood, and has recently been used in a window display in a vintage shop. It's a complete wreck, the fragile black lace on which the sequins are sewn having begun to crumble and tear. But it lives on, you see, in the fiction. I enjoyed describing it.

This story foregrounds one of my preoccupations with the new possibilities of women's lives in the middle of the twentieth century. It touches on creativity, sexuality, and pregnancy. It is also about the discovery of evidence of the past in attics and cellars. A student of mine recently said she was worried that her true story of finding in an attic bundles of letters written in a German prison camp was going to be a cliché. Well such clichés are what storytelling – fiction and non-fiction – has to work with sometimes. It's harder to make them come true in fiction. The image of the heart is also a powerful one in this story, as is the dreamy memory I have of Tasmania in spring, when the fruit trees are in blossom. My interest in art is also a key idea in the narrative – an idea that surfaces in several of the stories.

<u>HER VOICE WAS FULL OF MONEY, AND THEY WERE</u>
<u>CARELESS PEOPLE</u>

This story signals its own inspiration in its title – quoting from F. Scott Fitzgerald. Once I wrote a story that referenced Shakespeare, and a reviewer complained that because I was no Shakespeare I had no business quoting him. They get some funny ideas, the reviewers, and you can see that the comment hasn't stopped me from quoting. There is a theory, which seems more or less reasonable, that the literature you read nourishes your imagination and might even influence your morality. Is it reasonable? I wrote this story after tutoring some students on the text of *The Great Gatsby*. They were girls who were about to take their driving tests, who would soon be let loose on the roads behind the wheels of cars. The thing that gave me serious pause for thought was the fact that they endorsed the hit-and-run at the centre of the novel. I had the opportunity to suggest to them the idea that the thing to do at the scene of an accident is to stop, render assistance, call for help. But I think this idea went over their heads, even though the hit-and-run in the novel has the effect of leading to the death of Gatsby. They thought what Daisy and Gatsby did was the thing to do. So I wrote a piece of fiction.

This is one of the stories where I progressively chat to the reader about the plot. 'Who, you wonder, is driving the death car in our story?' It even has a choose-your-own ending.

THE CHRISTMAS TREE PLANTATION

I live in the small town of Castlemaine in the goldfields region of Victoria. So once upon a time this was a place of great excitement and hope, and also a place where greed gave rise to violence and death. As with many places in Australia, the melancholy of that

violence lies just beneath the surface of the land. I live near the
most forlorn cemetery you could imagine – called Pennyweight
Flat. In it lie the bones of many children who died in goldrush
times. A few of the graves are marked with old stones, but most
are not. And on the hill above the railway station sits, like a red
brick castle, the old gaol. Today it's the location of a delightful café with excellent smoothies and a magnificent view. Yet
under the ground beneath the prison lie, I believe, the bodies
of eleven men who were executed here. 'The Christmas Tree
Plantation' is in part a response to the violence and melancholy I
sense beneath the charming village that Castlemaine is today. It
is also a response to frequent news stories of young people who
go missing. There is an element of horrible fairy tale to such
reports, and the European pine forest, of which there are many
in rural Victoria, plays into that.

WAITING FOR THE GREEN MAN

The 'Life Saving' section begins with the internal story of the
wife of a clergyman. 'The empty heart at the heart of the full
life at the rectory was the absence of the child.' So there again is
the image of the heart at the heart, and the question of fertility
that infuses many of the stories, in 'Waiting for the Green Man'.
Deep down, it's a story about the wife's loss of faith, but it's also
about a miracle. The story is told by an omniscient narrator, but
it's inside Faith's secret heart, and the tone is calm, measured,
smooth, like the surface of Faith's life. There is the occasional
hint of a comment from the narrator, but this is always part of
the fabric of Faith's thoughts, observations and feelings. The
plot is ironic, but the tone is not. I think Faith is the only character in this collection that wonders about the nature of good and
evil, yet the whole collection really moves across that question.

Perhaps I have discovered the idea that links the stories. Yes? No? You may wonder what set this story in motion – well, towards the end of it there is a description of an incident in traffic. I confess that in real life I was the woman who stopped the traffic while the mother ran to the kerb with her baby. It was quite a strange experience, and it took the invention of the whole story of Faith to bring it to life. I have to say I love this story. Details such as the cannas, the roses, the spruce are from my own experience. I just wrote it in response to life, not for any special publication. One of the great things about writing fiction is that it gives you a way of reflecting on life, and of creating from your reflections. The story has never been published before, so I'm very pleased to be able to include it here.

HE PAINTED CUPIDS ON SOUP PLATES

'He Painted Cupids on Soup Plates' was written in response to an invitation to contribute to the Tasmanian literary magazine *Island*. Here was a chance to indulge some of my thoughts about Tasmania. A long time ago I realised that the name of the little town of Deloraine came from a character in a romantic Scottish poem. This fact was the inspiration for the story. Again the narrator has the freedom to chat to the reader from time to time about the content and structure of the story. I did enjoy locating Tasmania in place and time. Then I did something subversive which was to put a kind of Swiss finishing school more or less in the middle of nowhere, in 1955. The school is part of the fantasy of Tasmania, being in an old nineteenth century house that was built by a man who loved the works of Walter Scott. The fantasy of the school is doomed, and the story chronicles the tragedy. The contempt of the European princess at the end of the tale puts Tasmania, with all its romantic aspirations, in its place, with one flick of the lie that the princess tells.

GOING TO ST IVES

The final life-saving story, 'Going to St Ives', is a Tasmanian narrative, and it contains many facts from my childhood. I was so pleased that this story seemed to place itself naturally at the end, locating my heart of heart in the little island of Tasmania. It's embedded in nursery rhyme and myth, but the facts are perfectly clear. I discovered – if I had not known this before – that writing fiction can be more fun than writing memoir. This story is, in its odd way, memoir, but oh the freedom I felt as I detailed all these facts in this structure. It turns out to be a Second World War story, as well as a story about the private adoptions of babies by infertile couples. When I was reading it over, I found the discussion between the mother and the daughter to be particularly delicious. However fiction, which has and has not its rules, doesn't always require dialogue. I remember that this conversation just sprang into the story as I was writing.

This story and 'Think of Me' are the only ones here that had their origins in a photograph. Here it's a picture of the gracious Edwardian house, all long fancy windows and tall red brick chimneys, in which I was born. An odd thing is that the photo, unframed, is propped up among an untidy collection of random objects on the hallstand. That's where it lives. When the hallstand is dusted, the collection is reduced, but the photo slides back behind an iron hatpeg. The house in the picture was at the time a small private hospital. It looks nothing like a hospital. The fact that it was called St Ives has always pleased me, and seeing the picture set me off playing with the legend of St Ia who sailed from Ireland to Cornwall on a leaf, and also the funny nursery rhyme. Much of the story detail is factual, down

to the green felt mouse with which I entertained the babies –
and the life-saving incident could have happened, although the
narrative itself invented it. Private hospitals did sell babies to
infertile couples – but I am only speculating here about St Ives.
This is the fictional St Ives – which I could have renamed of
course, but then where would I be without St Ia on her leaf?

So that's the story, more or less, of where the stories come
from, and a little of how they were made. As I wrote about
them, I realised that so many of them had originated in one
object or observation which had then set off the chain of events,
the collection of characters, that became the narrative. Like it or
not, they do come from my own heart's core.

'The heart is deceitful above all things,
and desperately wicked:
who can know it?'
THE BOOK OF JEREMIAH, 17:9

ACKNOWLEDGEMENTS

Selected stories in this collection have previously appeared
in the following publications:

'My Hearts Are Your Hearts' *Antipodes* Volume 28 Number 1, 2014

'Diane's Fiancé's Ex-wife's Brother's Heart' *Australian Short Stories*
Number 29 Pascoe Publishing, 1990

'From Paradise to Wonderland' *Review of Australian Fiction* January,
2014

'Highway to Heaven' *New Australian Stories* Scribe, 2009

'My Beloved is Mine and I am His' *Antipodes* Volume 19 No 1, 2005

'Monkey Business' *Kill Your Darlings* Number 9, 2014

'No Through Road' *Wordlines* Hilary McPhee (ed.) Five Mile Press, 2010

'Where the Honey Meets the Air' *Australian Love Stories* Inkerman and
Blunt, 2014

'He Painted Cupids on Soup Plates' *Island* Issue 132, 2013

'Hare' *The Great Unknown* Angela Meyer (ed.) Spineless Wonders, 2013

'The Legacy of Rita Marquand' *Griffith Review* Edition 10, 2009

'Her Voice Was Full of Money, and They Were Careless People' *Best
Australian Stories* Black Inc, 2007

'The Christmas Tree Plantation' *Tailings* Volume 1 Number 1, 2015

'Back to the Womb' *Meanjin* June, 2015

'On the Mountains of the Moon' *Island* June, 2015